NEATH

R. Scott Bolton

Copyright 2022 by R. Scott Bolton
ISBN: 978-0-9997962-1-4

A Rough Edge Studios Production
www.roughedgestudios.com

Other books by R. Scott Bolton

From the Adventures of H. B. Fist
KILLED BY DEATH
OVERNIGHT SENSATION
BURNER

Brace Heller Novels
KNIFEPOINT
BEGIN RUMBLE STRIP

DEAD DICK

For Richard Senate.
Ventura County's Very Own Ghost Hunter.

As always, thanks to my ever-vigilant Quality Control Team. The readers listed below offered opinions and corrections that helped form the completed work, and I can never thank them enough for their input. But I'll try: Thanks to Shelley Bolton, Josh Bolton, Doug Bolton, Sue Bolton, John DeRuvo, Jeff Rogers, Steve Snider, and Denise & Joe Lopiano.

Also, a special shout-out to the National Novel Writing Month non-profit organization. Each November, they challenge their participants to write a novel in thirty days. I started in 2013 with this very book and have completed the first draft of a novel every year since. I heartily recommend NaNoWriMo to anyone who is considering writing a novel, screenplay, stage play, cookbook or whatever. NaNoWriMo helps keep you focused. Check them out and, if you're so inclined, donate!

www.nanowrimo.org

CHAPTER ONE

That jackass has the other two queens, thought Kyle Callahan. He glanced down at the five cards in his hands—two Queens, an ace, a three and a deuce—and then across the table at his current adversary, his co-worker Eddie Rivera. Eddie wore that same shit-eating smirk that he wore most of the time at the office. If Eddie had a poker tell, Kyle had yet to discover it.

The only other players, their wives, had long since folded out, and were chatting quietly on the sofa nearby, calmly paying no attention to the faux testosterone drama going on between their husbands.

Kyle narrowed his eyes, took another sip of Patron tequila from the shot glass in front of him (*one sip too many*, Kyle self-reprimanded) and then slapped his cards face down on the table in front of him.

"Fold," he said.

"You *chickenshit!*" Eddie laughed, and tossed his cards on the table, face-up. Kyle stared down at them. Not a queen in the bunch. Instead, two jacks stared back at him, seemingly with the same smirk as Eddie's. *Dammit!*

"That's what I'm *talking* about!" Eddie bellowed as he scooped up the pennies and nickels from the center of the table.

"Eddie!" scolded Eddie's wife, Gina. "You're going to wake the kids!"

"The kids have been asleep for hours," said Lisa Callahan, Kyle's wife. "And they sleep like the dead. It'd take a nuclear war to wake either one of them up."

"That's true," Kyle agreed. "Once I picked up Luke and held him upside down by his ankles, and that little turd slept right through it!"

Eddie laughed again. "One more hand?" he asked.

"Better not," Kyle replied. "I'm opening tomorrow, remember?"

Eddie nodded. He had asked Kyle to cover for him since Eddie was playing in a charity golf tournament the next morning. "Thanks for that," Eddie said.

"No worries, brother."

Lisa and Gina stood up and began scooping the party debris off the table. It took both to gather up all the empty wine-, beer- and shot-glasses there. Kyle and Eddie took care of everything else, crumpling up the empty snack chip bags (the crackle of cellophane was nearly as deafening as Eddie, Kyle thought) and folding down the tops of the bags that still contained chips. Kyle collected the cards, tapped them on the table to even the edges, and tucked them back in the box. "What's the big prize tomorrow?" Kyle asked.

"I don't care about the prizes," Eddie said. "I just do it for fun … and for the charity, of course."

"Right," Kyle said. "But you almost always win because you're this close to being a professional golfer. I mean, didn't you win a TV last year?"

Eddie laughed. "That was the year before," he said. "Last year I won those golf clubs."

"See? That's what I'm mean!"

"I don't know," Eddie said. "I'm a little rusty. I think I've only been out once since the tournament last year."

"Yeah," Kyle said. "But your rusty is still better than those other guys …"

A sudden blast of grinding noise and Lisa's startled yip of shock ended Kyle's sentence for him. He and Eddie rushed into the kitchen where their wives were standing by the sink. The grinding roar continued until Lisa swiped the wall switch for the garbage disposal.

"Are you okay?!" Kyle asked.

"Scared the shit out of me," Lisa said.

"Scared the shit out of *us!*" Gina added.

"What happened?" Eddie asked.

"Damn garbage disposal burned out, I think," Lisa said.

"Is there anything in there?"

"I don't think so."

"Keely's always dropping her spoon right down there," Kyle said, reaching through the rubbery sphincter of the sink and feeling around the greasy, moist mechanism there. A shiver ran through him as the image of the Dispose-All springing to life and shredding his fingers came into his mind.

As if on cue, a low rumble came from deep within the sink, and Kyle felt the mechanism start to move. He yanked his hand back sharply. The rumble vanished as quickly as it came.

"The hell was that?" Kyle asked.

"Must be a short," Eddie said.

"Great," Kyle said wiping the greasy moisture off his hands with a dishtowel. "Now we have a garbage disposal to replace. I thought we just put that one in!"

"It's been a few years, honey," Lisa said. "Probably time for a new one."

"How long have you lived here on Neath Street?" Eddie asked.

"Going on six years," Kyle said, marveling at the way time passed and the fact that his daughter, Keely, was born shortly after they had moved here from Oxnard.

"Been that long?" Eddie mused. "Doesn't seem that long."

"Was it new when you moved in?" Gina asked.

"The house?" Kyle asked.

"No, silly," Gina said. "The garbage disposal."

"Oh, no. The one that was here when we moved in was a piece of crap," Lisa said. "Kyle had to replace it right away."

"So, you got almost six years out of this one? Not too bad," Eddie said.

"Yeah," Kyle agreed. "Not too bad. I'll pick up a new one tomorrow and get it installed." He tossed the dish-towel onto the edge of the sink where it clung precariously until Lisa snatched it, folded it neatly, and tucked it in the handle of the stove.

"Okay!" Kyle said heartily. "I got to be at work in …" he glanced at the clock built into the microwave oven. "…

Just over four hours so, if you two will do me one big favor and get the hell out!"

"Kyle!" Lisa protested.

"Geett ouuut, geett out!" Eddie said eerily. "Just like that movie, huh? 'For God's sake, get out.'"

"Yeah, just like that," Kyle said, pointing at Eddie's chest. "For God's sake, get out. Otherwise, the house will be filled with flies, just like that movie."

"No problem," Eddie replied. "We *are* pest control experts, after all."

"That we are," Kyle said.

Eddie and Gina found their coats, slipped into them and they all said good night at the front door.

"Talk to you tomorrow," Eddie said. "Call me if you need anything."

"Will do. Good night, you two!"

The women gave each other a quick hug, and the Riveras headed out to their car, Gina guiding Eddie around to the passenger side and taking the driver's seat herself. The Callahans stood in the doorway and waved goodbye as their friends backed out of the driveway. Kyle watched until their taillights disappeared into the dark night, then closed the door and turned to his wife.

"That was fun," Lisa said.

"Yes, it was," Kyle agreed. "They are good people."

He pulled his wife close and kissed her gently on the neck.

"Wanna have some more fun?" he asked seductively.

"You're drunk!" Lisa said, giving him a quick peck on the cheek and tapping him on the nose. "Sober up and we'll try again tomorrow."

Kyle could only agree. He pulled off his clothes as he stumbled down the hallway toward the bedroom and was asleep the moment his head hit the pillow.

CHAPTER TWO

Kyle awoke at 6:15 the next morning, feeling crusty and groggy. He climbed stealthily out of bed, trying not to awaken his wife, and fumbled down the hallway to the bathroom. He turned on the light and winced at the bright glare and at the unhealthy scraping noise the exhaust fan was making. He sleepily brushed his teeth and shaved quickly and sloppily. *Hey, it's Saturday. Screw it.*

He went into the kitchen and through the door that led to the garage. There, he stripped off the launder's plastic from a fresh Jalama Pest Control uniform and reluctantly slipped into it. He pulled on his boots, filled his lunch box with a Bologna Lunchables and three Coca-Colas, and went back to the bedroom to retrieve his phone.

He kept the phone on the nightstand next to the bed where he also used it as an alarm clock. He grabbed the phone and, when he pushed the button to check for any messages, the lighted face illuminated something he caught out of the corner of his eye.

On his side of the exposed mattress (the blankets peeled away and folded back), was a small brown bug, about the size of an apple seed. *Is that a bed bug?* Kyle thought. Using the phone's screen as a flashlight, he leaned in and reached for the bug, his fingers poised like pincers.

The room suddenly went dark, the phone screen's maximum illumination time having expired. "Shit," Kyle whispered, flicking the button again and scanning the bed sheet.

The bug was gone. The sheet was empty, save for a few wrinkles. Kyle scanned the phone over the entire side of the sheet, looking over every exposed inch. After a few moments, he reached for the light switch, mumbled "Sorry, honey," and flicked on the lights.

Lisa groaned and mumbled, "What are you doing?" before quickly rolling over and going back to sleep. Kyle took the opportunity to inspect the bed closely, scanning the sheet and pillow carefully.

Nothing. No sign of a bed bug, a donut crumb, or a horse's head. Just nothing.

Kyle switched off the light, stood a moment, considering, then stuffed the phone into his shirt pocket and headed for his truck to go to work.

CHAPTER THREE

Kyle liked working Saturdays. Not every Saturday, of course, but the two Saturdays per month he was required to work were all right. On those days, a Saturday was almost like a day off. It wasn't nearly as busy—no one wants the pest control man at their house on the weekend—and the phone didn't constantly ring like it did on weekdays with customers demanding immediate service and the Home Office demanding answers and sales numbers.

Kyle was second in command at the local branch, the service manager to Eddie's Branch manager, so his every-other-Saturday schedule didn't bother him a bit. On Saturdays, there was only a handful of technicians out in the field and, even though they were spread sparsely throughout Ventura County, Kyle liked the fact that he knew exactly who he had in the field that day and pretty much where they were every minute.

Plus, the workday typically ended at 2:30pm instead of 5pm. Another bonus indeed.

But the best thing, as far as Kyle was concerned, was that Saturday was the day he could play his music as loud as he wanted while he worked. And that's what he was doing this morning at 7:30, blasting Black Sabbath on Pandora and whittling down the stack of paperwork on his desk to a manageable thickness so his catch-up work on Monday (there was always catch-up work on Monday) wouldn't be too crazy.

The day sailed along like most Saturdays do and, when the phone rang at 11:30am, Kyle muted "Paranoid" and answered on the second ring.

"Jalama Pest Control, Kyle speaking, may I help you?"

"What's up, brother?" It was Eddie. "How's your head this morning?"

"Been better."

"That's what all that beer and tequila will do to you. How's the day going?"

"Pretty easy, so far," Kyle said, mentally calculating that he had just under three hours left until he hit the "safe" zone. At 2:30pm, the main Call Center in Nashville would stop sending new jobs and that meant he could go home. The only way to ruin a perfectly good Saturday was to get an e-mail message at 2:15 informing him that a new customer wanted to start service at 4:30 that afternoon. Had to be done, although Kyle hated to give that dreaded job to anybody.

"Phones quiet?" Eddie asked.

"Yeah, pretty much. Got a couple of extra services set for Monday and I've cut the stack of concerns and updates down by about half. How'd the golf tourney go?"

"We took first place," Eddie said proudly.

"Of course, you did," Kyle said. "And I imagine you had low score again."

"Second place," Eddie said. "Bobby took first. He was on fire today. Couldn't have missed a shot if his life depended on it."

"So, what'd you win?"

"The prizes were a little cheap this year …" Eddie started.

"…but you do it for the charity," Kyle filled in for him.

"Yeah, that's right!" Eddie laughed. "I won dinner for four at Duke's in Malibu."

"Nice! I love that place."

"Yeah, thought I'd see if you and Lisa would like to join us. It's like two hundred dollars, man."

"Count us in. Lisa loves the Mai Tais there. They don't have the best beer selection, but if it's free, who am I to complain?"

"Got that right," Eddie agreed. "So, anything else going on?"

"Actually, yeah," Kyle said. "Let me ask you something. You ever bring a bed bug home?"

"You mean after a service?"

"No, I mean after a date. Of course, I mean after a service! You ever have one hitch-hike its way back to your house?"

"Not really," Eddie said. "I found one in my truck one day, crawling on my Tyvek suit, but I always strip down in the garage before I go inside. Gina launders that stuff before it goes anywhere else. Never found one in the house or even the garage for that matter. Why do you ask?"

"I thought I saw one on the bed this morning," Kyle said.

"Oh, shit, man."

"Yeah. I woke up, got ready for work, and when I went back for my phone, I thought I saw something on my side of the bed."

"Did you get it?"

"Well, no. Like I said, I only *thought* I saw something. I reached down to pick it up and then my goddamn phone went blank. When I lit it up again, the bug was gone."

"Probably seeing things, man. You strip down in the garage?"

"You know I do. Last thing I want is a case of bed bugs."

"Well, if you've got them, at least we know how to get rid of them."

"Yeah, but I don't want to do all that work. Pain in the ass, man."

"I know, I know. But if you've been careful, then you're not going to bring them in the house."

"I thought I've been very careful," Kyle said. "But I swear to God I saw one this morning."

"Are you sure it was a bed bug? Maybe it was a fly, or something."

"I suppose that's possible. It was still dark. Look, I'm not going to worry about it. I'll check the sheets tonight for blood or fecal matter but I'm not going to do a full-on inspection until I see something else."

"Makes sense."

"It was probably a fly. I didn't even think about that. Hard to see in the darkness."

Eddie laughed. "Maybe you shouldn't have told us to 'get out' last night? Maybe the flies are coming … you know, like the house in that movie."

"Yeah, I'm sure that's what it was, asshole."

"All right, man. I'll see you Monday. Have a good weekend."

"You mean have a good Sunday. You already screwed up my weekend."

"Hey, at least you get dinner at Duke's out of it."

"Yeah, there is that. See you Monday."

Kyle hung up the phone and stared at the computer screen, willing it not to signal new business until after 2:30pm. *If you can just hold off for another three hours...*

The phone rang again. Kyle noted it was ringing in on Line 4, the line that normally only rang when solicitors or recorded telemarketers called. "Hi, this is Judy from Carpet Care," they would say, "And we're calling to offer you a free two-room carpet cleaning, with the purchase of two rooms" or "Please hold: Your number has been chosen for a very special offer" or "This is an important call for Colson Samuels. If you are not Colson Samuels, please disregard this message." The latter was always Kyle's favorite. Samuels was a former technician who hadn't worked there for over three years, and collectors were still calling his old work phone to try and get paid.

Shaking his head, Kyle answered on the fourth ring. "Jalama Pest Control," he said. "This is Kyle. How can I help you?"

For a moment, there was only silence on the other end. "Hello?" Kyle said again. He was about to hang up when a high-pitched screech blasted out of the receiver, causing him to flinch and jerk the phone away from his ear. He stared at the receiver for a moment as the screeching sound rang throughout the silent office, and then slammed the phone into the cradle. The resulting silence was nearly as deafening as the sound had been.

"What the hell is up with that?" Kyle said to the telephone. It didn't respond, but only sat there silently. He stared down at it, expecting it to ring again. After about thirty seconds, Kyle shook his head and went back to his paperwork.

But the noise reverberated in his mind like a handball in a court. What the hell had that been? It didn't sound like the usual phone noise—like a fax line or digital feedback. It was a noise he'd heard before, but he couldn't quite put his finger on it. Finally, he just pushed it out of his mind and concentrated on his work.

Chapter Four

Kyle set the alarm, locked the office door and closed up shop at two minutes to three. He climbed into the cab of his Toyota work truck, started the engine, and then drove over the bridge and across the freeway to his favorite watering hole, a tiny little pub called Darryl's Couch, where the owner was the regular bartender and the eleven draft taps held some of the rarest craft beer in Ventura County. Kyle didn't get over to Darryl's Couch as often as he liked, but he allowed himself this indulgence on the Saturdays that he worked. One beer, a chat with Darryl, and he was on his way. It was a simple pleasure but one that Kyle cherished.

Today, Darryl was happy to tell Kyle that he had a new Stone Brew on tap, their latest anniversary ale and, like most Stone beers, it was hoppy and heavy and exactly what Kyle liked best. He sat at the bar and shot the shit with Darryl while he drank it down slowly, enjoying each and every sip.

After his visit with Darryl, Kyle stopped at Lowe's to pick up a few tools that some of the technicians had asked for. Two of them had lost their flashlights and, as Kyle always told them, a flashlight was the pest control specialist's most important tool. A few others needed new screwdrivers (for removing electrical outlets when dusting for roaches and ants) and one technician had broken his bump cap. Kyle would order him a fresh, logoed Jalama Pest Control cap on Monday but, for now, the guy needed something to protect his skull from protruding nails when he was checking attics for sign of rodents or other vermin.

It was just after five when Kyle returned home, parked his truck on the street and entered the back yard through the side gate. Even though he hadn't spent a moment in the field that day, he stripped down to his underwear on the outside walkway. He padded self-consciously past the chain link fence that separated his home from the neighbor's, came to the back door of the house and turned the knob. There, he deposited his work clothes directly into the washing machine.

Who knows? Kyle thought. *Maybe the office has bed bugs.* It wouldn't be the first time a pest control tech had brought home an unwanted guest after a job at a badly infested apartment complex or other residence.

Kyle closed the washing machine lid and slid open the pocket door that separated the washroom from the kitchen. The sweet smell of homemade cheese enchiladas wafted over him, and he felt a wonderful pang of wonder as to how he had earned such a treat. He stepped through the door and into the kitchen, snuggled up to Lisa at the stove and gently kissed the back of her neck.

"Enchiladas?" he said. "To what do I owe the honor?"

"Just felt like making them," Lisa said. "Why are you naked?

"Didn't want to bring any creepy crawlers in the house."

"Thank God for that."

"Where are the kids?"

"Keely's over at Emma's. You know. That new friend of hers," Lisa told him. "And Luke's over at the Sniders, playing Soldier of Fortune."

"Isn't that game a little violent?"

"No," Lisa said. "It's a *lot* violent. But it's a *game*. As long as he understands that."

"I think he does," Kyle said.

"I think he does, too," Lisa agreed. "And it's a shitload better than him playing Grand Theft Auto."

"Also, just a game," Kyle said.

"Yes," Lisa agreed again. "But a sick, twisted and profane game."

"Agreed. I'm gonna take a shower. Dinner almost ready?"

"Fifteen minutes or so."

"So, kids not gonna be home for dinner."

"Probably not. I told Keely I'd pick her up at seven and told Kyle he had to be home by nine."

"Perfect. More for me. I'm gonna take a shower."

Kyle showered longer than usual, enjoying the warm water in contrast to the chilly winter air. He toweled off and slipped into a pair of long pajama shorts and an old Motorhead t-shirt. They had no plans to go anywhere this evening. Some cheese enchiladas, one of Lisa's famous homemade margaritas, and some Netflix or Hulu. Sounded like a perfect way to spend Saturday evening.

He was surprised when he returned to the dining room to find dinner laid out and both of his children sitting hungrily at the table. Apparently, the magic of Lisa's enchiladas had not been lost on them, either. Keely sat at her end of the table, her blonde-haired Barbie laying prostrate by Lisa's plate. Luke sat beside her, his face buried, as usual, in his iPhone.

"Daddy!" Keely squealed when Kyle entered the room. She rushed out of her chair and threw her arms around her father.

Luke, of course, never even looked up.

Kyle encircled Keely in his arms. "Hey, sweet-cakes," he said. "How was …" He struggled to remember Keely's new friend's name. "How was …"

"Emma!" Keely told him. "Her name's Emma! It was fine, Daddy. We had fun, fun, fun!"

Kyle kissed the top of his daughter's head and then guided her back to her seat. He dropped heavily into his chair, just as Lisa brought him a very large margarita—on the rocks, rimmed with salt. Kyle's mouth watered at just the sight. His wife was famous for making some of the best margaritas known to humankind and Kyle had to agree. He often joked that was the main reason they had stayed married after all these years.

"How was your day, Luke?" Kyle asked his son. Luke, without looking up from the iPhone screen, simply shrugged. "That good?" Kyle replied, and then, after a moment, "Luke, put the phone down. It's time for dinner."

With a rebellious flare, Luke typed a few more characters into his phone and then dropped it noisily onto the table. Kyle bristled. Living with a teenager was like living with a coiled serpent. You didn't want to provoke it, but sometimes you felt like pushing it to the point of striking so that at least some of that pent-up energy would be expended. Kyle settled for a sip of the margarita and, as expected, its smooth citrus deliciousness was somewhat therapeutic.

Lisa returned to the table with a glass tray filled with cheese enchiladas and set it on the table beside a bowl of refried beans and another bowl of rice. She returned a moment later with a bag of plain tortilla strip chips, which she placed in the center of the table. "Let's eat!" she said, and Luke wasted no time in grabbing the ladle and scooping enchiladas onto his plate.

As they ate, Kyle watched Luke with some concern. The boy looked tired, his eyes encircled by mild, yet definite black rims. He was quieter than usual, too. Usually, Luke was full of stories about the kills he'd achieved in Soldier of Fortune as well of those of his friend Ricky, who was an expert in the game. Tonight, he simply ate— with the gusto of a fourteen-year-old, admittedly—but Kyle could still sense something was wrong.

In an attempt to bring up the subject without enraging the demon that lived inside teenaged boys, Kyle asked, "So, what'd you do today, Luke?"

"Nuthin," Luke said, which was exactly the answer Kyle expected.

"You didn't play that game all day, did you?" Kyle continued, knowing that it would not be a surprise if Luke answered yes. "I mean, it was a beautiful day. I hope you spent at least some of it outside."

"Yeah, I did," said Luke. "Went downtown with Ricky and his mom. Went through the thrift stores."

"That's always fun," Kyle said, thinking of Ricky's collection of vintage vinyl records, most of them purchased at thrift stores. "You find anything?"

"Nah, not this time," Luke replied, filling his mouth with enchiladas and falling quiet again.

"You should probably get to bed early tonight, son," Kyle said gently. "You look a little tired."

"I'm fine!" Luke snapped. He shot his father an angry look, grabbed his milk glass, drained it, and slammed it back on the table with a loud *thump!*

There's that demon, Kyle thought, *I better leave well enough alone. For now.*

When dinner was over, the children disappeared to their respective rooms while Kyle helped Lisa clear the table and then, as was per their agreement, Kyle did the dishes. The deal was that one of them made dinner and the other one washed the dishes. Kyle wished he could just rinse them and put them in the dishwasher, but Lisa didn't like the dishwasher, saying it never got the dishes as clean as she liked. Kyle had no such issue. Still, "a happy wife is a happy life," or so they say, and Kyle washed them all by hand.

At nine, Kyle tucked Keely into bed and read her a chapter from a tattered copy of Roald Dahl's "Charlie and the Chocolate Factory." They were just about to be introduced to the character of Willy Wonka for the first time and, although Keely proclaimed that she was excited about that part, she was sound asleep before the legendary candy man made his appearance. Kyle kissed her gently on the forehead, turned off the light and closed her door so that only an inch or so gap remained.

Kyle walked down the hall and stuck his head in Luke's room where he found his son, again, exactly where he expected him to be. Luke lay on his bed, fully clothed, texting on his iPhone.

"You okay?" Kyle asked.

"Yeah, fine," Luke snapped. "Close the door, would ya?"

Kyle nodded and did as his son asked. He knew that the demon lurked just beneath the boy's surface, and this was not the time to draw him out.

Lisa was on the couch in the living room and Kyle gave her a quick wink as he passed through to the kitchen to grab a beer. He opened the refrigerator and squatted before the lower crisper, where he stored what Lisa called his "fancy beers." Kyle hadn't been a beer drinker until recently, sticking to mixed drinks and fine tequilas, but the craft beer explosion had intrigued him and, after a few experimental tastings, he found that he loved the stuff. There were eight bottles in the crisper now: Firestone's Wooky Jack, Speakeasy's Double Daddy, Stone's Old Guardian and a few others. Kyle wasn't in the mood for the flowery hops of Double Daddy or the syrupy heaviness of Stone's barley wine, so he grabbed the Wooky Jack, a Black IPA with a mild bitterness and a tasty finish. He popped the cap with the opener on the refrigerator and poured the beer into a refrigerated glass. He had read somewhere that a non-refrigerated glass was better than a cold one because the cold one drew some of the beer's flavor away. After several experiments to test the theory, Kyle had dismissed that particular beer tip as nothing more than an urban legend.

He went back into the living room and sank into the broken-down La-Z-Boy chair that he'd received as a Father's Day gift a few years before. It was broken down, crooked and didn't lean back all the way but Kyle thought it was perfectly comfortable and had resisted getting a new one that may not be.

"What do you want to watch?" he asked Lisa, who was now prone on the couch, a book propped in front of her eyes, a pink fleece blanket covering her legs. Kyle noticed it was a new Jack Reacher novel, one of Lisa's favorites.

"Whatever," Lisa said. "I'm probably just going to read."

Kyle nodded, grabbed the remote and turned on the TV. He thumbed through the streaming apps—there were a lot of them—and selected HBO Max. He'd been catching up on *Boardwalk Empire*, a show he'd missed when it had originally aired, and one he found he particularly interesting. He sat back, sipped his beer and watched as Nuckie Thompson (played to perfection by Steve Buscemi) dealt with his batch of dangerous thugs.

He was about halfway through the hour-long episode when the effects of the long day and the Wooky Jack caught up with him. His eyelids had become heavy, and he could barely keep his eyes open, despite the nefarious antics of Nuckie and crew.

A delicate snore buzzed from the area of the couch and he turned to see that Lisa was already asleep, her Jack Reacher book folded open on her chest, rising and falling with her breath. Slowly and quietly so as not to wake her, he picked up the book and set it on the table, then opened the blanket and tucked it around her shoulders. Kyle whispered, "Good night, hon," and then walked down the hallway to the master bedroom where he fell into bed and was almost instantly asleep.

It seemed like only moments later when Kyle awoke. He was somewhat surprised to find that Lisa hadn't come to bed yet, but he could see the glow of the timer light in the living room and knew that it couldn't be quite two o'clock yet. Otherwise, that lamp would have turned itself off. He lay there for a moment, listening intently for whatever noise or disturbance it had been that woke him, when he felt something tickle his forearm.

His eyes darted toward the itch, and he felt something move there now as well. There, walking in little circles, were two apple seed-sized bed bugs, walking through the forest of hair on Kyle's arm.

Startled, Kyle gave a little yelp and smacked his hand down on the bugs and his arm. He leaped out of bed and rushed for the bathroom, turning on the faucet with his elbow and holding his arm beneath the running water. He slowly peeled his arm back away from his hand to find …

…nothing.

What the hell?

Kyle searched the back of his arm and his hand but there was no sign of the bed bugs. They must have scurried away before he could trap them with his hand. Little buggers could be very fast. Kyle went back to the bed, turned on the light, and pulled away all the covers, leaving the sheet exposed. There was no sign of the bed bugs. Not the bugs themselves, their fecal smears or the bloody signs of their feeding. Kyle spent the next hour doing a complete bed bug inspection, turning over the mattress, examining the seams, checking the lamps and nightstands nearby, even removing the pictures from the walls and examining the cracks and spaces in the frames. He even checked the Phillips screwheads in the doorway, remembering a story he had once heard of bed bugs hiding in the grooves therein. Still, everywhere he looked, there was not a single sign of bed bugs.

Screw this, Kyle thought. *I'll do a full bed bug treatment in this room tomorrow.* There was a rule in pest control that said you didn't treat for what you couldn't identify. Well, Kyle couldn't find any trace of bed bugs, but he sure as shit knew one when he saw one. He'd service the room tomorrow and, if necessary, any other rooms that showed suspicious signs as well. It'd be time consuming but well worth the result, cutting off the bugs' reproduction before they wound up with a real *infestation*.

Kyle stood there a moment and stared down at the bed, his eyes squinted in thought, when he suddenly became aware that someone was behind him, standing in the doorway. His skin goose-pimpled, he felt his breathing stop, and then he spun around to find Lisa standing there, staring at him sleepily. She blinked her still half-closed eyes, squinted at the tossed bed and upside-down mattress, and said simply: "I'll sleep on the couch tonight." Then she disappeared down the hall.

Kyle looked at the bed, shook his head, and decided there were worse places to sleep than in the broken-down easy chair in the front room. He turned off the light and headed to the living room.

CHAPTER FIVE

Kyle awoke Sunday morning, chilled by the lack of a blanket, groggy from a lack of sleep and cramped from sleeping in the La-Z-Boy all night. He glanced over at the couch where Lisa still slept peacefully, lightly snoring, her red-brown hair spilling over the edge of the couch and cascading toward the carpet. Kyle felt a little burst of love for her.

He wandered back to the bedroom, past the mess of a bed and into the master bathroom. As he enjoyed that first-of-the-day urination, he thought about the task ahead of him. He'd have to go back to the office, grab the necessary chemicals and tools, and then return to the house and do the full treatment, which could easily take two full hours.

The last thing he wanted to do was work on his only day off, but what choice did he have?

He finished peeing, stepped back into the bedroom and examined the bed. Not a shred of evidence that bed bugs had ever been present offered itself to the light of day.

I'm still going to treat it, Kyle thought, *but I'm sure as hell not going to do it today.*

He walked to the kitchen, poured himself a bowl of Count Chocula with milk (and was delighted there was still some in the box since Halloween was nearly a week ago) and returned to the La-Z-Boy. He snatched the remote off the table by the chair and turned on the TV. Even with the volume lowered, Lisa turned and moaned her disapproval. Kyle thumbed through the channels until he found Nickelodeon where SpongeBob and Patrick were immersed in another ludicrous adventure. As he laughed and enjoyed his Count Chocula, the revulsion he'd felt at finding bed bugs in his own home faded away and he and the family were able to enjoy the rest of their last peaceful Sunday for many weeks to come.

Chapter Six

It was almost 11:30 Monday morning when Kyle walked into Eddie's office and said: "Hey, I'm gonna take a long lunch today. Gotta go home and treat our bedroom for bed bugs."

"I thought you never found any," Eddie said.

"Saw two more last night," Kyle said. "Got away before I could grab them, but I saw them."

"Shit, maybe you took some home after all," Eddie told him. "Told you to be careful."

"I *was* careful," Kyle insisted. "I followed all the rules. I don't have any idea how they could have gotten in there." He paused. "Maybe one of the kids brought them home from a friend's. Keely's been hanging out with that new girl. Maybe she got them there."

"Then how'd they end up in your bedroom?" Eddie asked.

"I don't know," Kyle said and then, more frustrated, "I don't know! It's driving me freaking crazy. But if there are bed bugs there, I want to nip it in the bud, now."

"Don't blame you," Eddie said. "Sure, take a couple of hours and clean them out. Take one of those mattress covers, too. You need some help?"

"No, you stay here and run the ranch," Kyle said. "I'll be back as soon as I can. Thanks, Eddie."

"No worries, brother."

When Kyle got home, he immediately went to the still upside-down bedroom and swiftly began pulling off bedspreads, sheets and pillowcases. He carried them outside and left them in the hot sun, hoping it would get hot enough to kill any bed bugs that might be hiding therein but he was certain it wouldn't. He thought about putting them in the car or his work truck, where the temperature was sure to get up to the required 140 degrees but opted against it. If for some reason it didn't get hot enough, the car or truck would become just another carrier of the blood-sucking bugs. He'd leave them in direct sunlight for the time being and then make sure they were laundered in hot water before bringing them back into the house.

Back in the bedroom, he lifted the box springs out of the railings and took another close look at the cracks and grooves there. Nothing. No live bed bugs. No dead bed bugs. No nymphs. No fecal smears. If there were bed bugs in this room, they must have been very early into the infestation because they obviously had had no time to propagate. That was a good sign. He carefully sprayed the railings with a liquid pesticide and, while it dried, he inspected the underside of the box springs, its seams and edge. Again, however, he found nothing.

He had been into the job about half an hour when the house phone began to ring. Initially, Kyle decided to ignore it, and let it roll over to the answering machine, but for some reason the machine didn't pick up and the phone continued to ring. Aggravated, but concerned this might be a work call and Eddie needed help, he stomped over to the phone and snatched it off the nightstand.

"Hello!?" he said, a little more harshly than he meant to. There was a pause—a sure sign of an overseas telemarketer—but just as Kyle was ready to slam the phone down in the cradle, another familiar sound screeched into his ears.

It was the same noise he'd heard at the office on Saturday. That sickening screech that sounded like a dinosaur screaming. Kyle closed his eyes tightly in displeasure and slammed the phone back down, nearly breaking the receiver. "God *damn* it!" he cursed, and then wandered back to the center of the messy bedroom.

An hour later he had finished treating every possible area and was convinced that … if there were any bedbugs there to be found … they were dead or dying now. The bed-bug proof mattress cover was installed, any possibly infested areas had been sprayed and Kyle was certain he'd never done a more precise and complete job in all his years as a pest control specialist. He put the room back together as best he could, then did a quick scan of both Luke and Keely's room, again finding no sign of infestation. Finally, he gathered his tools and left the house.

Kyle returned his tools and chemicals to their places in the Tool-Tainer in the bed of his work truck and locked it up tight. He opened the cab door and was ready to climb in when something caught his eye. He closed the door and walked to the edge of the lawn, bending down and examining the grass there closely.

A small mound of gray dirt sprouted up from the grass there, surrounding the edges of a small hole.

"Just what I need," Kyle said aloud, "A goddamn gopher."

He scanned the rest of the yard and was thankful he saw no other signs of gopher activity. Hopefully, he'd catch this one sumbitch before it did any more damage. Kyle returned to his truck and re-opened the Tool-Tainer, withdrawing a boxed set of Easy-Set gopher traps. He set the trip plate, placed the trap it in the hole and led the attached chain about a foot away where he staked it into the grass. Pleased with the placement, he tossed the remaining trap and the now empty packaging into the bed of his truck and climbed into the cab.

He had just put his hand on the key in the ignition when, from inside the house, he heard the muted sound of the phone ringing again. *Screw it*, he thought, *they can leave a message this time.* He turned the key, the engine rumbled to a start and Kyle angrily backed out of the driveway, the tires giving a little screech. *Bed bugs, gophers and telemarketers*, he thought. *My house is going to hell.*

CHAPTER SEVEN

Tuesday night was Movie Night at the Callahan home, and this Tuesday was no exception. Kyle himself had come up with the concept, thinking it was a great way for everyone to get together, have a nice dinner, and then sit in the living room and enjoy a movie as a family. He was fond of saying, "I didn't buy a 52-inch television just to watch football," even though that was exactly what he had done.

Luke, of course, had rejected the idea of Movie Night at first, insisting on inviting over friends who did nothing but talk endlessly throughout the film or insult the choice of what they watched. That didn't sit well with Kyle who picked the films himself and was rather proud of the choices he made that catered to both the gritty action that Luke enjoyed but that weren't too offensive for six-year-old Keely. After a particularly noisy evening with Luke's friend Jerry—during which Jerry proclaimed of the first "Lord of the Rings" film that "only faggots would watch a movie with fairies in it,"—Kyle had put his foot down, making Movie Night *family only* night (not to mention banning Jerry from the Callahan residence permanently).

Luke threatened to boycott the evening entirely but, after being given no option but to sit through three or four films of his father's choosing, came to a grudging admiration for his dad's taste in movies. Although Luke preferred the more-violent action pictures of the aging Sylvester Stallone and Arnold Schwarzenegger (which, obviously, were not appropriate for Keely), Luke had to admit that films like the aforementioned "Lord of the Rings" series, as well as movies like one of his father's all-time favorites, "The Wonderful Ice Cream Suit," weren't half bad. And, although Luke still feigned disinterest during most of them, Kyle was always amused and satisfied to see his son immersed in one of the films he had chosen.

Tonight's movie was *Raiders of the Lost Ark*, a movie they had all seen, of course, but one they loved watching over and over again. Plus, there were leftover enchiladas from Saturday night's dinner, and nobody ever complained about leftover enchiladas. Kyle expected it would be a perfect evening … and it was.

Keely and Lisa cuddled up on the couch together, eating popcorn out of a Tupperware bowl. Keely leaned back against her mom in a time-travel double-image that proved beyond any doubt they were mother and daughter. Luke leaned dangerously far back in the La-Z-Boy chair, occasionally picking up his iPhone and texting a quick message to a friend or a tweet about the film. Kyle tolerated the use of the device here (he would not have tolerated it in a movie theater where others had paid a price of admission) as he sat in the bean bag chair in the middle of the living room, squarely in front of the TV. Kyle said he hated to watch a movie from an angle, and he thought the flat screen TV sound was much better when one was directly in front of it.

The movie ended at about 8:30, and everyone gave it a hearty thumbs up. As was usual procedure, they tidied up the living room together and then Keely marched off to her room to prepare for bed while Luke headed to his room and plopped down in the battered chair in front of the computer screen.

Lisa and Kyle went into the kitchen and did the dishes together, Lisa at the wash sink and Kyle drying the cleaned dishes and putting them in their respective spots.

"You know," Lisa said. "Technically, I made dinner, so it's really your turn to be doing these dishes."

"If that will get me enchiladas on a more regular basis," Kyle said, "I'll do the dishes every time."

Lisa laughed.

"Daddy!" Keely called from her bedroom.

"I think it's story time," Lisa said.

"I think you're right," Kyle agreed. He dried his hands, hung the dishtowel on the stove handle, and walked down the hall toward his daughter's room. He chanced a quick glance into Luke's room but could only discern that Luke was on the computer … whether he was on a porn site or a church site, Kyle couldn't tell. He assumed it was neither.

He stepped into Keely's room and was surprised to see his daughter sitting up in bed, her back against the headboard, staring with the kind of confused fear that a young child gets when they see something they can't explain and aren't sure how frightened they should be.

"Daddy," Keely asked. "What kind of bug is that?"

She pointed to the wall beside her bed and Kyle's eyes followed the invisible line her finger drew to a spot where he saw a brown, apple-seed-sized insect crawling slowly along the wall. As though it was aware of having been seen, however, the insect suddenly switched into high gear, and disappeared down along the crevice between the bed and the wall.

"Quick, honey, off the bed!" Kyle called. He grabbed Keely by the waist and pulled her off the bed, depositing her near the door, almost in the hallway.

"Daddy! What is it?" Keely cried.

Kyle yanked the blankets from the bed, examining them briefly before placing them in the middle of the room in a crumpled, pillowy mountain. He lifted the mattress away from the wall, making a taco shape out of it, and stared down into the crevice, his eyes straining to see any sign of movement in the darkness there.

Lisa stepped into the room, sweeping Keely into her arms. "Kyle?" she asked, concerned. "What's going on?"

"Quick, bring me the flashlight!" Kyle demanded. He was aware of his daughter's muted and confused sobbing and of Luke appearing in the doorway, too.

A few seconds later, he felt the cold heft of the old service flashlight they kept in the closet pressed into his palm and he flicked the light on, shoving it down into the space between the wall and the bed. He put his face as far down the space as he could, his eyes mere inches from the dusty carpet below. Scanning the flashlight back and forth along the path there, he searched for signs of movement, traces of dead bugs, fecal stains, whatever would lead him to find the bug he had just seen.

"Kyle, what's going on?" Lisa asked again.

"It was a bed bug," Kyle said.

"A *bed bug?!* How the hell did we get a bed bug?"

"I don't know," Kyle said. He let the mattress drop back into place and guided everyone out of the room. Keely continued to sob quietly. "But it's okay, everybody. This is what I do. I kill bed bugs. They probably snuck in on my work clothes. They're nature's perfect hitchhiker. But I know how to kill them, and I will. Keely, you'll have to sleep in the living room tonight…"

This brought Keely's half-hearted sobbing to a quick halt. "Yay!" she said brightly.

"But no TV," Kyle added, watching his daughter's shoulders slouch. "Or maybe you can sleep in Luke's room."

"No," Luke said simply.

"Either way, you can't sleep in here tonight. Go get your blankets, Keely, and we'll get you set up."

"Is it okay to get the book, Daddy?" Keely asked.

"I'll get it, honey," Kyle said. "You go get your bed made."

Keely went off to gather blankets while Luke went back to his computer screen. Lisa stayed behind, moving close to Kyle as he picked the Willy Wonka book off of the nightstand.

"What's going on?" she asked. "Do we really have bed bugs?"

"We got something," Kyle told her. "That's the fourth or fifth bed bug I've seen in the house over the past few days."

"How is that possible?"

"It's pretty easy to bring them home from work," Kyle told her. "But I thought I'd been careful. Every time we do a bed bug service, I strip outside the garage door and then go inside and dump everything into the washer." He paused. "You don't take it out again before you wash it, do you?"

Lisa was a bit put off. "No. Of course not. You may have been in the pest control business for twelve years, but I've been a pest control professional's wife for just as long. I know the routine."

"Maybe one of the kids brought them home from a friend's house," Kyle suggested. "Anyway, I treated our room this afternoon because I thought I saw some bugs there."

"You 'thought' you did?"

"Yeah, I never found any, though," Kyle said. "That's the weird thing. To see them running around on walls like that … they should be easy to find. I haven't been able to catch a single one yet."

"Great," Lisa said. "We've got a new strain of super bed bug living in our house."

"Don't tell the neighbors," Kyle said. "It'd be bad for business."

Lisa smiled sadly. "So, what are we going to do?"

"I'll treat the kids' rooms tomorrow," Kyle said. "If we keep having the problem, though, I'll have to get the heat team out here."

"Isn't that expensive?"

"Probably $3,500 or so" Kyle said. "But I can get us a pretty hefty discount."

"Let's hope it doesn't come to that."

"I'm hoping. Trust me."

Lisa was quiet for a moment. Then, she looked up at Kyle with a curious look on her face.

"You know," she said, tilting her head. "I think I've been dreaming about bed bugs for the past couple of days, too. How weird is that?"

Chapter Eight

Later that evening, Lisa Callahan was dreaming again.

She dreamed that she was floating down the hallway of her home just the way you do in dreams. The way Gumby and Pokey moved in those stop-motion animation programs. The way those smolderingly seductive vampires walked in the movies. Just gliding forward as though you were on a rail, your legs pressed together and still.

Lisa glided past Luke's room and paused a moment to look in. Luke was on the computer (of course) playing one of those alternate universe games where you ran around as a little pixelated character and interacted with other people running around as pixelated characters. Luke looked up and gave his mom a brief smile. She returned the favor with one of her own, the warmth of a mother's love shining behind it, and then floated down the hallway to Keely's room.

Keely was on the floor talking with her Monster High dolls, apparently preparing for an imaginary tea party. The dolls all sat in a semi-circle facing Keely, their painted eyes staring up at her with plastic adoration. Keely passed a tiny empty cup to the first doll (Lisa remembered the doll's name: Abbey Bominable) and then held up a finger. *One lump or two?*

Lisa watched her daughter drop invisible sugar cubes into Abbey's teacup (apparently, she had asked for two) and was hit by a brief wave of nostalgia. She remembered tea parties with her own dolls from too many years ago. Different dolls, of course, from a different era, but the tea parties were the same.

Keely looked up at her mother at that moment and gave her a carbon copy of the loving smile Luke had delivered only moments before. Lisa smiled back, again with that glow of motherly love, and then glided down the hallway toward the end of the hall, where the door to the bedroom she shared with Kyle yawned open, its black mouth yielding no secrets as to what waited inside. Lisa slid to the door and pushed it open gently. Like magic, the lights inside went on and she could see.

The room was a mess. Laundry from every family member was strewn across the floor in what to the casual observer would look like random piles. Lisa thought she was probably the only person in the world who could identify the four individual piles there: One for Keely's clothes, one for Luke's clothes, one for her husband's and one for her own.

The bed was rumpled and unmade and, as Lisa glided closer, she saw why. Kyle was tucked into his side of the bed, the blankets pulled up to his neck, his face the loose-skinned mask of someone deep asleep. A glittery shellac trail of saliva oozed out of the corner of his mouth and formed a dark dime on the pillow below. Lisa felt another burst of love, but this time for an adult companion, her best friend and her longtime lover. She sighed deeply and glided closer to the bed.

She couldn't say why, but she suddenly felt exhausted. It didn't make any sense, especially with Keely still up and playing with her dolls. Lisa never went to bed before Keely, not even when she was sick, but now she wanted nothing more than to climb into bed beside Kyle, spoon into his human warmth and sleep there until morning. She reached down and pulled back the covers, which came away so lightly they seemed to be made of air, and she gave a little yip of terror as she found the bed filled to spilling with seething bed bugs.

There were hundreds of them, thousands even. They crawled over each other in a hideous mass, their sheer quantity giving them the look of a massive writhing scab. A wall of them adhered to Kyle's naked back, each swelling to fullness with the man's life blood and then dropping off so that another could take its place. Tiny legs squirmed everywhere, like a million electrocuted worms.

Lisa wanted to drop the covers and run but found herself frozen in place. Even as the bugs arched up and over the underside of the blanket, racing for the edge and toward Lisa's exposed hand, she found she could do nothing but stand and stare in horror. There was a scream trapped in the back of her throat but her windpipe had constricted to a pinpoint so she could neither breathe nor make any sound.

But when the first bug touched her hand, the spell was broken. Lisa threw down the blankets and spun in a dizzying 180, gliding out of the room as if on a greased rail and racing down the hallway at high speed. She moved so fast that there was no way she could look into the children's rooms as she zipped by ... *but she did* ... only to find her ten-year-old daughter still playing with her Monster High dolls despite the fact she was coated by a skin of wriggling bed bugs. Only to find her son casting a digital spell on another digital player, perfectly comfortable in his M&M shell of writhing, hungry bed bugs.

Then Lisa was past them, gliding fluidly at speed to the other end of the hallway where the door to the kitchen was *supposed* to be ...but wasn't. Instead, the hallway came to an abrupt dead end. Lisa scrabbled along the wall where the door should have been but wasn't. It was gone! There was no trace of it! The only way out was to go back the way she came. She did another 180-degree turn and felt her heart catch in her throat as she saw that the hallway was *filling* with bed bugs. They were pouring out of the master bedroom door like a dirty brown river, filling the hallway like that scene from Stanley Kubrick's *The Shining*, when the elevator doors opened and a tsunami of blood flooded out until the lobby was painted with gore.

The bugs poured down the hallway at her, rolling and roiling as though they were one animal instead of thousands and, although she knew it was impossible, she swore she could hear the gnashing of their terrible tiny teeth.

Lisa spun on her dream-lubricated axis and beat her fists on the wall where the kitchen door should have been. She felt her knuckles bruise, then split. Slim ribbons of blood spattered the wall in front of her and she knew in her heart that the bed bugs, those apple-seed-sized vampires, would sense the blood and come even faster.

And then, abruptly, the wall was gone. The kitchen entrance gaped open, and Lisa fell through, her arms flailing. She braced herself for a jarring impact with the hard kitchen tile and was stunned when she felt *grass* beneath her, warm from the midday sun. She found herself spread out, face-up, on the front lawn, her limbs twisted beneath her at impossible angles. Strangely, impossibly, she felt no pain.

She pushed herself up on her elbows and stared fearfully back at the house, expecting a boiling sea of bed bugs to be pouring down upon her, scrabbling across her with their spindly legs, gnawing at her with their flesh-boring mandibles.

But all she saw was her house, the house she had fallen in love with the moment she laid eyes on it, all those years ago. The house she now shared with her husband, their son and their daughter. Her family. The house she called home. It looked peaceful and calm from where she sat on the lush green lawn. Serene, in fact. Exactly how a *home* should feel.

But inside, she knew, inside there was *evil.*

CHAPTER NINE

Lisa jerked awake and found herself staring wide-eyed at the ceiling, her heart pounding in her chest. *Jesus Christ,* she thought, *what was that all about?* She had told Kyle that she'd dreamt of bed bugs, and she had. But in the previous dreams, there had only been a few, crawling in twos and threes on the walls and individually on laundry items and food stuffs. Not in a seething river that made the zombies in World War Z seem tame by comparison.

The clock on the nightstand read a digital green 2:35am. Lisa's mouth felt like someone had poured sand in it and her throat was a dry gully. For a silly moment, she was embarrassed that she'd been laying there on her back, breathing through her mouth and snoring like a chainsaw. A glass of water sounded like a little bit of heaven to her. She let her heart settle for a few moments, and then gently peeled back the blankets so as not to awaken her husband. He was already freaked out by the few bed bugs he'd seen and the last thing she wanted to do was tell him about her dream … scratch that … her *nightmare*. Softly, she set her feet on the floor and stood up.

She stepped out of the bedroom and into the dark hallway. Her eyes had adjusted to the lack of light, but it was still difficult to see in the achromatic early morning. Lisa felt her way down the hallway, her skin creeping as she passed Luke's room, then Keely's room, visions from her dream flashing in her head. Finally, she entered the kitchen.

She padded to the sink and felt more than saw the empty glass in the wire dish rack on the right side of the sink. She filled the glass with water, hoping the running stream wasn't too loud, and then drank the entire glass down in one long gulp. Her mouth felt wonderful as it hydrated, and her throat lost that dry roughness that made it difficult to swallow.

Lisa returned the glass to the rack and headed back to the hallway. Her eyes had adjusted even better to the darkness now so she could discern shapes, edges and contrasts well enough that it was much easier to maneuver back toward the bedroom.

She was walking past Keely's room when she heard her daughter moan softly in her sleep. It didn't sound like the moan of a looming nightmare but more like someone trying to have a conversation in their sleep. Smiling at the thought of it, Lisa backpedaled and pushed open Keely's door, thankful for the tiny nightlight plugged into the outlet near her daughter's bed. For a brief second, her mind flashed again on the image from her dream; that of her daughter playing with her Monster High dolls, covered in vibrating bed bugs. She pushed that image away and looked down at her daughter's bed.

And her breath caught in her throat and her heart rabbit-thumped in her chest.

Because there was a woman standing by the foot of her daughter's bed. A pale woman, wearing a black dress with a lacy white collar, her long black hair tied back in a conservative bun. She stood at the foot of Keely's bed staring down at the girl with a look of concern on her alabaster face, her fingers laced together over her abdomen. Occasionally, she gave a little sigh as she watched the little girl sleep.

Lisa felt her skin crinkle into goosebumps and the soft hairs at the back of her neck rose up. It was as though she were back in her nightmare. Her throat felt as if her windpipe had shrunken to the size of a drinking straw, and she couldn't draw breath. She wanted to scream for her husband, to scream for him to come *now* but, although her mouth was working, her throat wouldn't allow her voice to make a sound.

But in a millisecond that all changed when Lisa's fear transformed into pure rage. Her mouth stopped working and became a twitching line of pure anger. Who was this person and what was she doing in her house? *And what the fuck is she doing by my daughter's bed?!*

An animal growl finally escaped from Lisa's throat, and she launched herself at the woman, who calmly looked up and acknowledged her. Lisa hit her with the force of a football tackle and they both went down hard. Something snapped briskly as they crashed to the floor, but Lisa wasn't sure whether it was the interloper or herself.

Lisa pushed away from the floor, her head spinning wildly, her eyes blinded by rage, her body aching in a dozen places. She was just climbing to her knees when something hard and heavy fell on top of her, cracking her on the head and bringing stars to her eyes.

Then the room was suddenly bathed in light and Keely was screaming and Luke was saying, "Mom? Mom? Mom!" and Kyle was standing over her, lifting off the sliding closet door that had been knocked off the hinges and crashed down on top of her.

And Lisa wondered *Where is she? Where is the woman by Keely's bed?*

Kyle's face, lined with concern, was suddenly before her, his fingers pushing the hair out of her eyes and brushing away what Lisa knew must be blood but was in fact only sweat from her sudden exertion. "Lisa? Lisa! Are you all right? What the hell's going on? What are you doing?"

Where is she? Lisa thought, *Where's that woman?*

Her vision started to fade as she tilted toward unconsciousness, but her fading rage wouldn't let her go. "The woman." she managed. "There was a woman in here."

"Someone was in here?" Kyle said. He turned to Luke. "Luke, go check the house. Make sure all the doors and windows are locked."

Luke disappeared down the hallway and returned a moment later with a baseball bat in his hands. "I'll yell if I find her," he said, and rushed out of the room.

"Who was it?" Kyle asked Lisa. "Who'd you see?"

"I don't know," Lisa said, forcing herself to her feet. "I didn't recognize her." Images of Elizabeth Smart and her kidnappers sprang chillingly to her mind. "Kyle, what was she doing here?"

Luke re-appeared in the doorway. "House is locked up tight," he reported. "Doors and windows both."

"Did you see anything?"

"No." He shrugged, a little guiltily. "Nothing to see."

Lisa closed her eyes and shook her head. She glanced around the room, at her daughter sobbing on the bed, at the closet door broken off the hinges, at her husband and son looking down at her with confusion and worry.

"Honey," Kyle said carefully, "Are you sure?"

"Yes, I'm sure!" Lisa snapped. "I saw her. She was standing right here! I knocked her down!"

Kyle looked doubtfully around the room. "Honey," he said gently. "There's nobody here. What were you doing up, anyway?"

"I just wanted a glass of water," Lisa said. Once again, she looked into the faces of her family, saw the doubt and confusion there. She glanced around the room and saw no trace of the woman she was certain she had tackled like a rugby player. She looked at the broken closet door, which was almost exactly where the woman had been. And she felt the tears coming. Tears of frustration and embarrassment.

"I know what I saw ..." she said weakly. And collapsed into Kyle's arms. sobbing. He put his hand behind her head, holding her comfortingly against his shoulder.

"I know you did," he said gently. "Maybe you were just tired. Maybe you were still half asleep."

Lisa shook her head against his chest. *No, I wasn't,* she thought. *I know what I saw.*

They stayed that way for a few moments, and then Lisa sighed deeply and pushed herself away from Kyle. "I'm fine," she said. "Maybe I was mistaken. Sorry, everybody."

Kyle ordered everyone back to bed and, when Keely complained about sleeping alone, Lisa volunteered to stay with her. She climbed into bed with her daughter as Kyle and Luke wandered back to their respective bedrooms. A few minutes later, the lights clicked off and the house was once again dark.

Keely snuggled up to her mother and was asleep within seconds. Lisa did not sleep. Instead, she lay on the bed, staring up at the ceiling, her ears prickling for any night sound that didn't belong.

Chapter Ten

Morning took forever to arrive and still came too early. Lisa slept not a wink but managed to get up with the kids and help them get ready for school. She was stiff and sore from the incident of the early morning, but not so much that she couldn't function. It helped that Kyle, normally at work at 6:45am sharp, had decided to go to work late today, getting the kids' lunches made and making sure their backpacks were full of the things they needed. Perhaps more importantly, he had already made a pot of coffee. Lisa poured herself a cup and sat at the kitchen table. She knew Kyle wasn't a coffee person. He was a soda guy, first thing in the morning and throughout the rest of the day, so the coffee probably wouldn't be very good. This morning, she really didn't care.

Lisa heard the front door open and close and then Kyle entered the kitchen and sat down at the table beside her.

"Kids on their way," he said, taking a sip. "How you feelin'?"

"Shitty," Lisa said. "I'm sore, I'm tired, and apparently I'm seeing things."

"I know you saw *something*," Kyle said. "Never thought I'd see the day you'd use that hard head of yours as a battering ram."

That made Lisa smile a little. "Tell you what," she said. "If that bitch was in there, she's feeling it today."

Kyle laughed. "Well, I already fixed the door," he said. "It just hangs on a groove there, and you just knocked it out of the groove." He opened the fridge and grabbed a Coke Zero Sugar. "You calling out sick today?"

"No. In fact, I'm gonna take a shower and get the hell out of here." She stretched her sore arms and was pleased to find they felt better already.

"Okay," Kyle said. "Call me if you need me." He stood up, gave his wife a quick peck on the cheek, and headed for the door. He had just touched the doorknob when Lisa called from the kitchen:

"Honey?"

"Yeah?"

"Tomorrow let me make the coffee, okay?"

CHAPTER ELEVEN

An hour later, Lisa felt a thousand times better. The hot shower had not only washed away the sweat and pain of last night's incident, but it had washed away some of her fears, too. The woman in Keely's bedroom seemed to be part of a fading dream now, and Lisa found herself doubting her vision more and more as the morning went on. Maybe she *had* been half asleep. Maybe the shadows from that damned nightlight had tricked her mind into seeing something that wasn't there.

But Lisa could remember the apprehensive look on the woman's face, and the startling alabaster color of her skin. If her mind had been playing tricks on her, they were *really* good tricks. *We're talking Penn & Teller tricks here,* Lisa thought.

She slipped into her Souper Salad World uniform and made sure the "Manager" badge was straight and even with the seam. She didn't mind the uniform so much. It looked more like a pants suit than those polyester dress thingies the servers had to wear. And the company cleaned them for her, so she saved a lot of time on laundry, the one household task she truly hated.

The truth was she *had* thought about calling out sick, but Souper Salad World was rolling out a new product today: the Choco-Bacon muffin. Lisa was always amused at the fact that she worked for a huge restaurant chain that prided itself on its buffet of fresh salad and wholesome soups, yet it was the freaking muffins that drew everyone through their doors. And there were high hopes about the Choco-Bacon muffin, a dark chocolate muffin with bacon bits inside instead of chocolate chips. Lisa knew that many of her customers today would be smuggling extra Choco-Bacon muffins into their pockets and purses to take home and eat later. That was supposed to be a no-no, but Lisa knew that the company really didn't care and, so, neither did she.

She had just grabbed her keys off the table and was heading through the kitchen door to the garage when the phone rang. Her shoulders slumped. She had been that close. Had she left just three minutes earlier, she'd have been well on her way to work by now and not bothered by what was probably an annoying telemarketer. Even as she turned on her heel to go back and answer the phone, she thought about just ignoring it and going on her way. *But what if it's work?* She thought. *Or one of the kids' schools?*

She answered it as the third ring died in the air, half hoping that whoever was on the other end had given up and hung up themselves.

"Hello?"

SCREECH! The noise blasted out of the phone at such a high volume that the little speaker in the receiver crackled. Lisa jumped, dropping both her phone and keyring.

The phone fell halfway to the floor and hung there, like a condemned man on the gallows, while the keyring skittered to the floor and slid beneath the refrigerator.

"Dammit!" Lisa grabbed the dangling receiver and held the phone to her mouth. "Fix your phone, asshole!" She slammed it back on the hook.

Dropping to her hands and knees, Lisa peered under the refrigerator. Fortunately, the keyring was in easy reach, and she snagged it with her fingernails and pulled it out. She ran the keys under the faucet for a moment to clear away any unwanted gunk and then dried them with a kitchen towel.

This time, the doorbell rang.

Her shoulders slumped again. *You gotta be kidding,* Lisa thought. She tucked the keyring into the pocket on her uniform and was halfway to the front door when the bell rang again.

"Coming!" Lisa said, turning into the main hallway and coming to a dead stop.

Through the frosted glass of the front door window (actually five pieces of glass, spread out like a peacock tail) Lisa could see her visitor's outline.

And it bore a striking and chilling resemblance to Keely's visitor from a few hours before.

Lisa stood still for a moment, and the doorbell rang once more. That initial chill of fear transformed again into anger and Lisa stormed toward the door, her face twisting in a grimace, as she yanked it open, and stared down into…

…into the face of her 80-year-old neighbor, Mrs. Trellis.

"I'm sorry to bother you, dear, but would you happen to have an extra cup of sugar," Mrs. Trellis said in her watery voice. She held up a glass measuring cup with her two palsied hands. "I'm fresh out and I can't have my morning coffee without my sugar, you know!"

Morning coffee at 11:00am? Lisa thought. "Of course, I do," she said, taking the glass cup. "Give me just one minute."

Mr. and Mrs. Trellis had lived next door when the Callahans had moved to Ventura nearly six years ago. While they weren't exactly fast friends due to the age difference, they had always been good neighbors and, when Mr. Trellis had passed away after suffering a debilitating stroke two years ago, the Callahans had taken Mrs. Trellis under their wing. Lisa was in a hurry to get to work this morning, but she wouldn't say no to Mrs. Trellis just because she was running a little late.

Lisa rushed into the kitchen, opened the cupboard and grabbed a box of sugar. She rapidly and sloppily filled Mrs. Trellis' cup and all but ran back to the front door. She had just stepped into the hallway when the floor gave a little lurch and she felt herself being lifted slightly. Her hand shot out to brace her body against the wall and she was aware of the glasses rattling in their cupboards. *Earthquake?* It was over as soon as it started, and she thought of her elderly neighbor standing alone in the doorway.

"Mrs. Trellis? You okay out there?"

There was no response. Lisa got her feet underneath her and rushed to the front door where Mrs. Trellis stood happily, her hands extended to receive the blessed cup of sugar.

"Thank you, dear," Mrs. Trellis said, taking the cup. "After I have my coffee, I'll feel human again."

Lisa stared at her neighbor, confused. "Didn't you feel that?" she asked.

"Feel what?" Mrs. Trellis answered.

"That earthquake…" Lisa said and realized she might be overstating it. "That *tremor*. Didn't you feel it?"

Mrs. Trellis shook her head. "An earthquake?" she said. "No, dear. I didn't feel anything."

Of course, you didn't, Lisa thought, *with that palsy you're shaking enough already*. Immediately, she was ashamed of herself. "Must have been my imagination," she said quickly. "Enjoy your coffee!"

"I will now!" Mrs. Trellis said. "Have a good day, dear!" And she turned and hobbled off the porch.

Lisa shut the door behind her and stood for a moment, her head cocked in curiosity. She had already apparently seen a ghost standing in her daughter's room. Why should it surprise her that she had imagined an earthquake? She rubbed her face with her fingertips, massaging the temples. Not that earthquakes were so rare here. Hadn't she read somewhere that California had nearly thirty earthquakes each day? Of course, the vast majority of those were so minor that the citizens never felt them and maybe that was the case here. Maybe she had felt one of those minor earthquakes that only a few people actually feel. And Mrs. Trellis was old and palsied herself. What was a little more shaking to her? Pushing that thought out of her mind with a little self-admonition, Lisa glanced at the clock and realized it was already 11:11; she was due at work in less than twenty minutes. Those Choco-Bacon muffins wouldn't wait! She locked the front door, made sure she had her keys (they were still in the pocket of her uniform) and went out the kitchen door into the garage.

The Camry started easily, like it always did, and Lisa used the remote clipped to the sun visor to open the garage door. She backed the car out into a beautifully sunlit day.

As she checked both left and right before backing out into the street, Lisa glanced over and noticed there had been a little gopher activity in the front yard since she'd last looked. There were at least three or four gopher mounds now protruding from their well-tended lawn. Lisa made a mental note to tell Kyle—a *licensed pest control professional* as he liked to say—to get his act together and make sure the gophers caused no more damage. Then, she straightened the wheel and pointed the nose of the Camry toward work.

Chapter Twelve

Kyle Callahan reached out and used his thumb to squish a reddish-brown bed bug against the oh-so-white wall of his current customer's home. The bed bug offered him a satisfying wet pop as it burst against the wall, splashing the contents of its body, swollen with its host's bodily fluids, against the wall in what looked like a miniature of an unedited crime scene photo. He wiped the decimated remains on his Tyvek suit, leaving a smear there that Dexter Morgan would have been proud of.

"Get that little bastard?" asked Kyle's best friend and supervisor Eddie Rivera.

"Yeah, I got him," Kyle said. "This place is swarming with them." He wiped the sleeve of his Tyvek suit across his profusely sweating forehead. So far, the heat crew had managed to crank the temperature up to a baking 120 degrees. It wasn't hot enough to kill bed bugs yet, but it was hot enough so that Kyle and the other technicians were miserable with the thick, cloying heat.

"Liquid wouldn't have done shit here," Eddie said. "We're gonna have to come back a couple of times to follow-up on this one."

Eddie was talking about treating this particular bed bug service again with a liquid pesticide after the current heat treatment was completed. A liquid-only treatment was effective, but not as effective as the much more expensive heat treatment, which included an automatic liquid follow-up anyway. Kyle had to agree. A liquid treatment at an infestation this severe would have led to a cyclical nightmare of recurring visits. At least the heat treatment would wipe out most of the bed bug population the first time, with the liquid follow-ups taking care of the rest.

Kyle felt a little tap on his back, and he turned to find Eddie holding a solitary bed bug pinched between two fingers. "Had one on your back," Eddie said.

"That's how the little bastards hitchhike home!" Kyle said bitterly.

"Exactly," Eddie said. "By the way, how's that going? Home, I mean." To which he immediately followed with: "Let's get the hell out of here. Too goddamn hot."

Both men maneuvered past the fans and heating devices, exiting the front door and walking toward their work trucks outside. Eddie peeled open his Tyvek suit, revealing his Jalama Pest Control uniform underneath. "Man, it was freaking hot in there!" he said.

"Got that right," Kyle replied, peeling his suit open like a lobster on a dinner table.

"So, what's up with the bugs at home?" Eddie asked. "Did you get them all?"

"I *think* I did," Kyle said. "Tore our bedroom apart and treated the kids' rooms pretty thoroughly." He paused thoughtfully. "Weird thing is that I still haven't seen one."

"You haven't *seen* any?" Eddie asked, incredulous. "Brother, you don't *have* any, then."

"Well, I've *seen* 'em," Kyle clarified. "A couple of times, now. But I haven't *caught* any."

"See any dead ones?"

"No. Not a one."

"Then you don't have them."

"Eddie, I've *seen* them," Kyle said hotly. "I've seen them in our bed, and I saw them in Keely's room. I know they're there!"

"Maybe you're seeing things," Rivera said. "Been drinking too much of that fancy craft beer."

Kyle laughed. "Well, that part may be true," he said. "But I know what I saw." He paused, thinking of Lisa's comment from earlier that morning. "You know what else is weird," he continued. "Lisa said she saw something, too."

"Lisa is seeing bed bugs, too?"

"No ... well, I don't think so. At least she hasn't told me if she has. But last night, I was sound asleep, man, I mean in a freaking *coma*. And all the sudden, Lisa's in Keely's room, screaming her goddamn head off. "

"What?!"

"Yeah, she's in Keely's room and she's screaming, so I leap out of bed and, like I'm there in four seconds flat, and Luke's already in the room, and Lisa's on the floor in a heap. She ran into the freaking closet, using her head like a goddamn battering ram. And she's mumbling about this *woman* who was standing at the end of Keely's bed."

"What the hell was she doing in the closet?"

"She wasn't *in* the closet. She tried to tackle this woman, whoever it was, and crashed *into* the closet."

"But there wasn't anybody there?" Eddie asked.

"No one," Kyle replied, "No one but me, Luke, Keely and Lisa."

"Was she sleep-walking or something? Maybe she only *thought* she saw this woman."

"That's what I told her," Kyle said. "And you know what she told me?"

"No. What's that?"

"She told me that she knows what she saw."

Eddie laughed. "Isn't that what you just said about the bed bugs?"

"Yeah," Kyle said soberly, "It is."

"Maybe your place is haunted," Eddie said. "Time to call those Paranormal Activity guys on TV."

"Very funny," Kyle said. "We've lived there over five years with no problems. What happened? Did we suddenly grow an Indian Burial Ground below us or something?"

"Maybe they didn't realize you were there," Eddie said. "Finally played that heavy metal you love so much too loud, got their attention."

Kyle laughed. He reached down into his boot and dug his fingers beneath the edge, finally reaching the spot just above his ankle where an itch had begun, scratching it as best he could from this awkward angle.

He felt the swelling there, knew from past experience what it was.

"Goddammit," Kyle said miserably. "Something just bit me."

CHAPTER THIRTEEN

The new Souper Salad World Choco-Bacon muffins proved to be the tremendous success their corporate creators hoped they would be, and Lisa Callahan was stunned as she looked down at her watch to discover it was nearly 9pm. Her workday should have ended over an hour and a half ago. Having served hundreds of diners, most of them senior citizens, for almost nine full hours, Lisa was bone tired. Still, she allowed herself an amused smile as she watched a woman, eighty years old if she was a day, pull a large plastic baggie out of her purse and fill it with—not only Choco-Bacon muffins—but sourdough rolls and a couple of foil-wrapped baked potatoes.

"We should stop her," said Brenda Taylor, Lisa's Lead mid-day Server. "That's just not right."

Lisa sighed. "No, it's not," she said. "But if the company doesn't care, I don't care. And, really, I'm too tired to give more than half a shit right now."

Brenda laughed and went to check on the pasta section, which looked to be running low on capellini.

Lisa quickly surveyed the dining room to confirm everything was going smoothly and then walked briskly toward the back room, smiling and nodding at the Choco-Bacon muffin-munching customers as she did so. She poked her head into the office where Souper Salad World's manager, Cal Rosen, sat behind a glowing computer screen, pretending to crunch sales numbers but secretly browsing Craigs' List.

"Hey, Cal, I'm out of here," Lisa told him. "See you tomorrow."

"You opening or closing?" Rosen asked her.

"I'll be in for breakfast," Lisa said.

"How we doing on Chock-Bakes," Rosen asked, proudly using the nickname he had coined for the popular new item.

"We've got plenty," Lisa told him. "You couldn't have placed a more perfect order, Cal. We're selling the crap out of them, and we've got plenty for the rest of the week."

"Very good," Cal said, clicking away on the mouse in front of him. "Have a good night."

"You, too." Lisa closed the office door behind her and walked quickly to her car, unpinning the "Manager" badge as she did so. The best thing about the company manager uniform was that, once the name tag was removed, it did a reasonable impression of a decent pants suit for non-restaurant business. In other words, Lisa could go out for a drink after work.

She plopped heavily into the Camry's front seat, grabbed her cellphone from the cubby just behind the emergency brake, and dialed Gina's number. Gina answered on the first ring.

"Are we on?" Gina asked.

"We're on," Lisa confirmed. "Kyle's home with the kids and I *really* need a drink."

"I was hoping you'd say that," Gina said. "Larsen's?"

"Perfect."

"Okay," Gina said. "See you in fifteen."

Lisa folded her phone, started the car, and backed out of her parking space. As she drove, she had a pleasant debate with herself over whether she was drinking Chardonnay tonight, or Grey Goose vodka with cranberry.

CHAPTER FOURTEEN

Gina was already sitting at the bar, drink in hand, when Lisa walked in. Lisa hung her purse on the hook beneath the bar and took the seat beside her.

"You didn't waste any time," Lisa told Gina.

"No, I didn't," Gina said. "I've been looking forward to this all day. Right after you called, I told Eddie 'I'm outta here' and hot-footed it over!"

Lisa laughed. "What are you drinking?" The reddish liquid in Gina's glass wasn't the Chardonnay or Grey Goose with cranberry that Lisa had been craving, but it looked pretty damned good ... maybe even better.

"Mai Tai," Gina said with a mischievous giggle.

"Oh, you're going *big*," Lisa laughed.

"Told you. I've been looking forward to this all day!"

The bartender appeared, flashed Lisa a bright smile and asked, "What can I get you?"

Lisa eyed Gina's Mai Tai, wondering if she could manage one of those and still function for breakfast shift in the morning. "A glass of Chardonnay," she told him.

"No, she *won't!*" Gina exclaimed. "She'll have one of these Mai Tais. Fix it up for her!"

Lisa laughed. "No, I've got to work in the morning," she said. "I'd better have a Chardonnay."

"You don't want a Chardonnay," Gina said. "You want a Mai Tai. Make her a Mai Tai."

The bartender, whose name tag, Lisa noticed, read *Hi, I'm Danny*, flashed that smile again. "I make a pretty good Mai Tai," he said.

Lisa laughed, then nodded. "Oh, okay then," Lisa said. "Make it a Mai Tai."

"That's my girl!" Gina exclaimed.

Danny wandered off to make her drink. Lisa sighed. "Oh, what a day," she said.

"Oh, that's right!" Gina said. "Chocolate Bacon Muffin Day!"

"Choco-Bacon," Lisa corrected. "Or Chock-Bake if you're Cal Rosen."

"Chock-Bake? Oh, that's a great name," Gina said sarcastically. "Tells you just what it tastes like: chalk."

"They're not bad, actually," Lisa told her. "I mean, you've got to like chocolate and bacon, but they taste surprisingly good together."

"I saw a bacon chocolate bar at Vons," Gina said.

"Yeah, Kyle got one of those. He liked it."

Gina took another sip of her Mai Tai as Danny delivered Lisa's drink. Lisa picked it up and had a sip. "Mmmm. You were right. You do make a good Mai Tai."

"I wouldn't steer you wrong," Danny told her. "Let me know if there's anything else you need." And off he went.

"So, Kyle told Eddie you had a strange visitor last night," Gina said.

"Kyle should learn to keep his damn mouth shut," Lisa complained. Kyle was going to hear about this. He didn't need to be spilling their life secrets out to the entire world.

"You know those two," Gina said. "They tell each other everything."

"I know," Lisa said, still seething.

"Well?" Gina prompted. "What happened?"

"It was nothing," Lisa said, shaking her head. She unconsciously put her hand to her forehead where there was still a small bump from her encounter with the closet door.

"It was *something*," Gina said. "Eddie said Kyle told him you knocked a door off the hinges, or something."

Lisa bristled. *There* was the problem with Kyle shooting his mouth off. The Telephone Game effect, when the real story gets turned into something completely different by the time it goes through three different sets of ears.

"I didn't knock a door off its hinges," Lisa said. "It was the closet door. I just bumped it and it fell off its grooves."

"Holy shit," Gina said. "What was that all about?"

"I thought I saw somebody," Lisa said. "I *did* see somebody. Standing there in Keely's room."

"What?!"

"Yeah. I got up to get a drink of water and, as I walked by Keely's room, I saw this ... this woman, standing there by the foot of Keely's bed, looking down at her."

"Who was it?"

"I have no idea. Never saw her before in my life."

"What was she doing?"

"She was just standing there. Looking down at Keely. She didn't seem, you know, *dangerous*. She just stood there looking down at Keely like she was worried about her or something."

"What the hell!" Gina exclaimed.

"Scared the shit out of me, at first," Lisa went on. "But then it kinda pissed me off, you know. Like, *what is this woman doing in my house, in my daughter's room!* So, I just kinda rushed her, tackled her."

"Did you get her?"

"Well, no. I thought I hit her but, when the boys came running in, she was long gone."

"How'd she get away?"

"I don't know. I don't know how she could have. And then Luke checked the house, and all the doors and windows were locked. I don't know how she got in or how she got out."

Gina took another sip of her Mai Tai. Lisa noticed it was already half gone and was a little shocked to find that hers was nearly as emptied.

"You were probably half asleep," Gina said. "Probably just the shadows or something."

"I know what I saw," Lisa said, a little more sharply than she meant to. But the alcohol was having its effect and Gina didn't catch the tone.

"I'm just sayin'," Gina said. "Maybe you only *thought* you saw a woman there."

"I saw her," Lisa said. "She was wearing a black-and-white outfit and her hair was drawn back, away from her face." She took another sip, a bigger sip, of her Mai Tai. "And she had the pastiest skin I've seen in long time."

"Girl, you got a ghost!" Gina laughed. "Your place is *haunted!*"

Lisa froze for a second, bristled again at Kyle and his big fat mouth, and then laughed nervously. But she really hadn't heard anything remotely funny. The fact was she had considered that possibility already. She could still picture the woman staring down at Keely, and the image was so clear, so vivid, that Lisa was certain she'd seen the woman there. So certain, in fact, that, rather than believe what she saw was only shadows and reflection, she had allowed herself to entertain the thought of her home being haunted … and of the woman being a ghost.

Thinking these thoughts in the bright lights and homey comfort of Larsen's Grill, with her best friend Gina by her side and an attractive young bartender named Danny bringing her Mai Tais, made Lisa feel silly and stupid. She hurriedly drank down the last of her Mai Tai and signaled Danny to bring her another. "Split it with me?" she asked Gina.

"Does a bear poo in the woods?" Gina replied.

Lisa felt a pang of guilt for having another of the delicious, alcohol-heavy cocktails (even if in fact she was splitting it) but she also felt that she had never needed another one so badly.

CHAPTER FIFTEEN

Kyle Callahan was in the bedroom, laying on his back and watching TV. He glanced over at the clock on the nightstand there. In just thirty minutes, it would be midnight. The kids were in bed, and Kyle assumed they were both asleep. Well, he knew Keely was out like the proverbial light—she'd gone to sleep almost the second he'd finished reading the latest chapter of *Charlie & the Chocolate Factory* to her—but he wasn't so sure about Luke. For all he knew, Luke was still lying in bed, wide awake, listening to the latest Led Zeppelin soundalike at a dangerous volume and reading one of those graphic novels he liked so much, probably one about zombies. *Well, at least he's got good taste in music,* Kyle thought, a*nd he got that from me!*

Lisa hadn't made it home, but Kyle wasn't concerned, at least not yet. Wednesday was Lisa and Gina's Girls Night Out, and they usually stayed out late. Not often quite this late, but it wasn't time to start calling the hospitals just yet.

Kyle took another sip of the Makers Mark in the highball glass on the bedside and was careful not to dribble it on his pajamas (a pair of skull-emblazoned basketball shorts and an old Black Sabbath t-shirt). He savored the whisky's caramel burn and then grabbed the remote and turned the television volume up, just a notch, so he could better hear Jimmy Kimmel's opening monologue.

He reached down and gently rubbed the back of his ankle where he'd been bitten by some sort of insect, probably a bed bug at the godforsaken job he'd done today. The bite had swollen to about the size of a small grape, and it itched so much that it hurt. Kyle resisted the temptation to scratch. The last thing he wanted to do was add insult to injury with some kind of infection. He thought of an old friend of his, John Decatur, who'd once suffered a minor spider bite that had turned into a full-blown staph infection. Decatur had spent eight days in the hospital and, at one point was in a full-blown coma. Kyle remembered visiting Decatur in the hospital and thinking there was no way he was going to come out of it. Eight days and a $100,000 hospital bill later, however, and Decatur had been released.

Kyle thought ruefully how the doctors had informed Decatur he'd been bitten by a brown recluse spider when Kyle, a well-trained and state-licensed pest control expert, knew that was next to impossible. There were no brown recluse spiders in California, except those very few that managed to hitchhike from the Southeast, and they were few and far between. It wasn't the bite that normally made people sick; it was the infection that followed. And that was exactly what had happened to Decatur.

Jimmy Kimmel was just getting to the meat of it when Kyle heard the front door open, and Lisa's keys clanked into the bowl near the front door where she usually kept them. A few minutes later, she stepped into the bedroom and said, "Well, hello there, sailor." The "s" in sailor was a little thick and Kyle knew she was feeling no pain.

"Hello back," he told her. "I see you guys had a good time tonight."

"I only had a drink and a half," Lisa said, and chuckled. "But they were Mai Tais!"

"Good thing you don't have to work tomorrow," Kyle said.

"I *do* have to work tomorrow!"

"I know," said Kyle. "How'd the Choco-Bacon muffins go over?"

"How do you *think* they went over," Lisa said. "This is America! If there's anything we love, it's chocolate and bacon!"

"And beer," Kyle added.

"And Mai Tais!" Lisa said and laughed again.

Lisa began sloppily stripping out of her uniform, dropping the pieces to the ground willy-nilly, something she would never have done when cold sober. She unhooked her bra and let it fall to the floor, and then stepped out of her panties. Kyle lay on his back, enjoying the show, pleased that his wife's nakedness still turned him on so much. A moment later, she was in bed beside him, her naked warmth pressed against him, and he felt himself rising to the occasion. "How was *your* day?" Lisa asked him, and then her mouth was on his and he took her in his arms and soon they were one.

Kyle awoke hours later, a still naked Lisa by his side. It was pitch dark now (Kyle had climbed out of bed and turned off all the lights after their lovemaking) and he wondered what it had been that awakened him. Then his ears caught the final settling of what must have been the bottles in the bathroom cabinet, and he thought, *Is someone in there?*

Before that thought could completely form itself, however, the bed gave a lurch as the entire house shook on its foundation, and Kyle could hear not only the bottles in the bathroom cabinet shaking and rattling but the chatter of dishes in the kitchen, like little glass teeth gnashing. A low rumble filled his ears.

Earthquake!

Kyle leapt out of bed and ran to the door. He knew it wasn't a good idea to try and move during an earthquake, but he felt the need to get to the kids' rooms, to make sure they were safe. He tumbled into the hallway to see a sleepy-eyed Luke standing there already, looking frightened and confused.

Then, like so many earthquakes seem to do, it just ended. The house stopped vibrating and the rattling and ringing sounds of jolted items faded. The thundering rumble tapered and disappeared.

Kyle looked at his son and said, simply, "Earthquake. You all right?"

Luke nodded. Kyle walked down the hall and peeked into Keely's bedroom. His daughter was still sound asleep, the quake and its accompanying din never disturbing her. Kyle smiled. He'd always said that his kids slept so hard it'd take a nuclear war to wake them ... and here was the proof.

But the earthquake *had* awakened Luke, who still stood in the doorway by his room, his eyes betraying his shock and surprise at being roused out of bed by a shaking house. "Go back to bed, son," Kyle told him. "It was just a little earthquake. We're fine."

Luke nodded almost imperceptibly, and then stumbled back into his room.

Kyle returned to his bedroom, where Lisa still slept, perfectly undisturbed. *Like mother, like daughter,* he thought. He re-arranged the blankets around her and then climbed into bed himself. He grabbed his iPhone off the nightstand, activated it, and thumbed through the apps until he came to an icon with a graphic that looked like the planet Earth splitting in two. QuakeStat was an informational app that claimed to report every earthquake around the globe. Kyle had downloaded it just for fun but had been disappointed that all the action seemed to happen on faraway islands with Tahitian sounding names. If that had been an earthquake here now—and, really, what else could it have been?—QuakeStat, a "real time earthquake updater" according to its creators, should be reporting it any minute.

Fifteen minutes later, laying in the dark, anticipating another quake or aftershock and staring fruitlessly at QuakeStat's "Latest Action" screen, Kyle finally succumbed to the sandman, and fell into a deep sleep.

He was awakened four hours later by Lisa's terrified scream from the hallway. "Kyle! Kyle! Wake up! Now!"

Chapter Sixteen

Kyle burst out of his bedroom door and into the hallway to find Lisa and both kids standing there, staring at him, their eyes wide with fear. He gave each of them a quick once-over to make sure no one was hurt and then looked at Lisa questioningly. She pointed to the hallway wall behind him.

There, written across the top of the wall near the ceiling, were the words: *You must leave this house now!* in perfect, almost classroom-precise letters. Kyle felt a cool chill go through him. He read the words again, and then again more slowly. Finally, he turned back to his family.

"Who did this?" he asked angrily. He wasn't accusing anyone there in the hallway, but his sudden shock and anger made it seem that way. He saw Lisa bristling.

"Well, none of us did," Lisa said sharply. "Somebody was here in the middle of the night—while we were *sleeping*—and did it. And I don't think it's very funny!"

Keely began to softly cry.

"Luke, do you know anything about this?" Kyle asked.

"No!" Luke protested. "Why would I know anything? I didn't do it!"

"Did you have any friends over last night?"

"No! I was in my room alone! I didn't do anything!" Luke said sharply, his brow furrowing. Kyle was aware that the teenager demon was about to make an appearance. "What's your problem?"

"I'm just saying …" Kyle began.

Keely's cries began to grow louder.

"Don't worry, honey," Kyle told her. "It's okay."

"It is *not* okay," Lisa spat. "I told you there was someone in the house the other night, but you didn't believe me. But now we know, don't we?"

"Lisa, I'm sure this is some kind of joke…" Kyle began.

"Great fucking joke!" Lisa cried. "A real laugh riot!"

"That's enough!" Kyle said. "Lisa, you need to calm down."

"Don't tell me to calm down!"

"You *need* to calm down," Kyle said again, nodding in Keely's direction. Keely's crying continued to intensify.

Lisa stared at Kyle with hard eyes, and, for a moment, he was sure she wasn't going to back down. But then she looked at her daughter, saw the tears and the fear there, and slowly nodded. "I know," she said after a moment. "I'm just a little scared and upset, okay? Come here, honey." She held her arms out and Keely came running to her, burying her face in her mom's neck. "It's okay, baby," Lisa cooed. "Everything's fine."

Kyle looked up at the writing on the wall again. *You must leave this house now!* What the hell did that even mean? And who could have written it? Kyle tried to force himself to remember coming through the hallway during the earthquake. Had the writing been there then? Had he just missed it in the dark? He couldn't be sure.

"When did you first notice this?" Kyle asked. Lisa joined him as they stared at the scrawled warning on the wall, Keely now quiet in her arms.

"Luke saw it first," Lisa said. "When he came out of his room this morning."

"Was it there during the earthquake?" Kyle asked Luke. "Did you see it then?"

"Earthquake?" Lisa said. "What are you talking about?"

"No," Luke said. "No, I don't think so. At least, I didn't see it."

"I know," Kyle agreed. "I didn't either."

"What earthquake?" Lisa said impatiently.

"A little one, last night, while you ladies were sleeping the sleep of the dead," Kyle said. He gave his daughter's nose a little pinch and was rewarded with a smile, a smile he was very grateful for. "No big deal," he continued. "Rattled some plates, shook the pictures on the walls, but nothing broken. I'm sure you'll see it on the news today."

"I didn't feel anything," Lisa said doubtfully.

"Like I said, it wasn't a big deal," Kyle said. "But it was noticeable. Right, Luke?"

"Woke me up," Luke said.

Kyle stared at the letters on the wall for another second and then said, "All right. Enough of this. Let's get ready for school everyone!" He turned toward Lisa. "Honey, why don't you help Keely get ready and I'll clean this up."

"Clean it up?" Lisa asked.

"Yeah, can't leave it there," Kyle said carefully, indicating Keely again. "While you two get ready to go."

Lisa read the look in Kyle's eyes. "Okay," she said. "Sounds good." She touched the back of Keely's head. "Let's go, honey."

The two of them wandered back into Keely's bedroom.

"You, too, Luke," Kyle said and waited until Luke had gone back into his room, too.

Kyle crept forward and stared closer at the writing on the wall. The walls in the hallway were painted a light brown and the substance the words were written with was a pale, almost grey/white color. If the wall had been much lighter, he wouldn't have been able to make out the words at all. He peered closer, trying to determine what the substance was, but the words were too high, written just an inch or so below the ceiling line.

Kyle padded into the kitchen and grabbed the step stool there. He dropped it in the corner of the hallway and climbed up, putting his face as close to the writing as he could. The words were written with near perfect form in some kind of powdery white substance that Kyle recognized but couldn't quite put his finger on. He had already stepped down from the stepstool and, in fact, was taking it back to the kitchen when it dawned on him.

Chalk. The words were written on the wall with chalk. *You must leave this house now.*

Suddenly, unbidden, an image of Eddie at the poker party the other night flashed into Kyle's mind. "Get out! Geeet oouuut!" quoting the scene from that horror movie (was it *The Amityville Horror?)* when both of them, all *four* of them for that matter, had been well into their cups. Had Eddie done this? Would he have played a practical joke as thorough as this? Had he snuck into the Callahan's home after dark and written those words on the wall?

Kyle dismissed the thought it almost instantly. It wasn't that Eddie never took part in any practical jokes. He and Kyle had pulled off some masterpieces together at the office. But Kyle couldn't imagine Eddie breaking into someone else's home just to play a silly joke. Plus, Kyle had seen plenty of examples of Eddie's handwriting on service tickets, contracts and the like, and, while it was generally neat, it didn't come close to the precise, linear letters he saw on his wall now. But, if Eddie had really been focusing …

Kyle pushed it from his mind. It wasn't Eddie, couldn't be Eddie. But then … who else could it have been?

Kyle was just reaching for the telephone to call the police when it rang before he reached it. "I got it," he called out automatically and grabbed the phone from the receiver.

"Hello?" he said, and was greeted by that same blast of noise, that screeching scratch from the office that had set his nerves on edge and sent goosebumps running up and down his spine.

He spat an unintelligible curse and slammed the phone back into the cradle. *I wish they'd fix that, whatever the hell that is,* he thought. He picked up the receiver again, gingerly listening to make sure the screeching sound was gone, and dialed the local police.

CHAPTER SEVENTEEN

Christ, I hope that thing doesn't collapse underneath him, Kyle Callahan thought, watching the rather large police officer balance on the small wooden stepstool like an elephant in a circus act. *I don't know what that thing's rated for, but it's not three hundred pounds!*

The officer, whose nameplate Kyle read as "H. Farmer," was eyeing the mysterious graffiti as though he were a handwriting expert, moving his head from the subject to the predicate and staring at the letters with what appeared to be great interest. This despite the fact he was a good six inches shorter than Kyle, seventy pounds heavier and peered through a pair of cheaters perched on the tip of his nose like Santa Claus.

"You say this wasn't here last night when you went to bed?" Farmer asked.

"No," Kyle told him. *For the third time*, he thought.

"And what time did you go to bed?" Farmer asked.

"About 11:30, I guess," Kyle said. "Jimmy Kimmel was just coming on."

"Jimmy who?" Farmer said, coming down off the step-stool to the carpeted floor of the hallway.

"Uh, Kimmel," Kyle said. "Late night talk show host."

"Oh-uh," Farmer said, which Kyle interpreted as "Uh-huh," as in the positive response. "Never seen him. I'm a Fallon man, myself."

"I like Fallon, too," Kyle told him.

"Never be anybody like Carson, though," Farmer said. "He was the best, and probably always will be."

"I guess so," Kyle said.

"Letterman was all right," Farmer continued. "Got a little too weird for me sometimes. And don't even get me started on that Conan character. Something wrong with that red-headed stepchild."

Kyle, hoping to steer the conversation back onto the right track, asked, "So, have you ever seen anything like this before?"

"Like Conan?" Farmer asked, wide-eyed. Kyle realized he might as well have asked *How many of your children have gills like a rainbow trout?*

"No," Kyle replied, impressed with his ability to keep exasperation out of his tone but not sure how much longer that would hold out. "The writing. The graffiti. Have you ever seen anything like that before?"

Farmer looked back over his shoulder, and, for a moment, Kyle thought for certain the man had already forgotten why he was there. But Farmer surprised him. "Well, I've seen lots of graffiti, that's certain enough, but I can't say I ever saw anything like this. Doesn't seem malicious to me, more like some kind of a joke. You say you've got teenaged children?"

"A boy. Fifteen."

"That's more'n likely your problem right there," Farmer stated.

"He said he didn't do it," Kyle said.

"Well, what did you expect him to say?" Farmer said. "But maybe he didn't. Maybe it was one of his fool friends. You remember what it was like to be fifteen, don't you?"

"Of course," Kyle said. "But my idea of a prank was more like stealing a guy's shorts in gym, and running them up the flagpole, or filling the punchbowl with liquor."

Farmer laughed. Kyle gestured at *You must leave this house now!*

"I don't even know what that *means*," he said. "Or who would think it was funny."

"You ever see that show, *Family Guy*?" Farmer asked.

"Um, yes, I have," Kyle said, wondering if they were diverting to another television program review.

"Do you think it's funny?" Farmer asked.

"Not particularly," Kyle replied.

"But I bet your boy does, doesn't he?"

Kyle didn't have to think long on that one. Luke watched *Family Guy* religiously, often laughing so hard, one had to wonder if he hadn't been at the nitrous oxide first. "Yes, he does," he said.

"My point exactly. What one person finds funny, another doesn't understand. Like Letterman and that Conan guy, you know what I'm saying?"

Kyle had to agree. "I guess you're right."

"Now, I can go downtown and come back with a fingerprint kit, if you're really concerned about this," Farmer said, jerking his chin up at the chalked warning again. "But I'm very certain this is just a joke. Not a very funny joke, someone coming into your home in the middle of the night and writing on your hallway, but a joke nonetheless." Farmer sucked on his teeth for a moment. "Just like that *Family Guy.*"

"So, what do I do?" Kyle asked.

"Wait it out," Farmer said. "Odds are, whoever did this is going to spill the beans. They're dying to know if you got their joke. All the same, make sure all the doors and windows are locked every night."

"They were!" Kyle protested.

"Make sure," Farmer said firmly. "Every night, right before you go to bed. And I'll send a patrol around every couple of hours, kinda keep an eye on things. You see anything funny, or any more of this ..." He jerked his head in that direction again. "...give me a call and I'll come running. But, honestly, Mr. Callahan, I don't expect anything to come of it."

Kyle extended his hand and Farmer's meaty paw enveloped it. "Thank you for your time, officer," Kyle said. "I appreciate you coming out."

"No worries," Farmer said. "That's what we're here for." He took a deep breath through his nose and then continued. "I see you're one of those pest guys, aren't you?"

"That's right," Kyle said. "I work over at Jalama Pest Control."

"What do you recommend for ants?" Farmer asked. "I get 'em in my bathroom sometimes and I can't get rid of the little buggers."

CHAPTER EIGHTEEN

As it was every year, when winter began, the pest control business slowed down. Bugs just didn't flourish like they did in the summer and, when they seemed to disappear from local homes, customers excitedly assumed their pest control worries were over, never considering that their creepy crawly problems would be back in throngs in just a few months when spring and summer rolled around again.

Normally, this annual slowdown was cause for concern for Kyle Callahan. It meant more hours out of the office and more time out in the field, trying to drum up new business by knocking on doors and visiting commercial properties (especially those listed on the Health Department's Restaurant Closure website). And it meant more harping on his technicians that, as important as doing a professional and thorough service was, it was just as important to make new sales and to grow the business.

However, when he arrived at work that morning, for once he was thankful for the winter reprieve. His ankle was killing him where the bug bite was, and the snug fit of his steel-toed boots wasn't helping any. He stopped in the small office kitchen, grabbed a Coke Zero out of the refrigerator and then sauntered into Eddie's office. He fell into the visitor's chair and promptly removed his boot and began rubbing his injured foot through his socks.

Eddie didn't even look up from his computer screen. "Sure, make yourself comfortable," he said, "Kick off your shoes, put up your feet."

"Dude, that bite is freaking *killing* me," Kyle told him. He peeled off his sock and rubbed the back of his foot. The bite seemed to have swelled to the size of half a golf ball. It was warm to the touch, and it itched like there were a thousand tiny worms inside, all squirming constantly as though to get a better position. Kyle tried to get a look at it, but the bite was badly placed. All he managed through all that awkward bending and twisting at weird angles was to prove that there was no way he could see the bite clearly without the use of a mirror.

"Damn, boy, your feet reek!" Eddie complained, finally taking his fingers off the keyboard and holding them to his nose.

"I know. Sorry," said Kyle. "Damn waterproof boots don't only keep water out, they keep sweat in." He rubbed his foot as he spoke, occasionally mewling in pain. "I've never had a bite like this," he said. "It hurts like a bruise or something and it feels like it's gonna burst."

"Probably not a bed bug, then," Eddie said. "You do a flea job or something else recently? Spiders? There've been plenty of black and brown widows this season."

"I don't know," Kyle said. "It's possible. It's just weird that I first noticed it at that bed bug service yesterday."

"Could've happened before we got there."

"Yeah. Could have."

Kyle put his sock back on, wincing as the edge slipped over the throbbing bite, and then forced his foot into its boot, cursing softly as he tied the laces. "Hey, Eddie," he said, after a moment. "Let me ask you something."

"Ask away."

"Does the phrase 'You must leave this house now'" mean anything to you?"

Eddie stopped typing again and stared across the desk at Kyle. "No," he said. "Should it? What's it from?"

"I was hoping you knew," Kyle said. "When we woke up this morning, somebody had written that in our hall-way."

"What?"

"Yeah. Right along the ceiling line. *You must leave this house now.* In chalk of all things."

"What the hell are you talking about?" Eddie asked.

"It's like graffiti, or something," Kyle told him. "It wasn't there when I went to bed at about 11:30, and it wasn't there when that earthquake woke me up at about two."

"What earthquake?" Eddie asked.

Kyle's face scrunched up in disbelief. "Are you serious, man? You didn't feel it either?"

"No. I didn't feel any quake last night. I think you might have been high." He laughed and shook his head. "You holding out on me, brother?"

Kyle ignored the joke. "Lisa didn't feel it, either," he said. "Or Keely for that matter, not that she ever would've. But it woke up both me and Luke."

"Couldn't have been very big," Eddie said. "I didn't see anything on the news."

"It was big enough to rattle the dishes in the cabinets," Kyle told him. "But, yeah, I guess it wasn't that big. Anyway, when Lisa went into the kitchen this morning, that's when she saw it." He paused. "Actually, I think Luke saw it first."

"Graffiti? In the hallway?"

"Yeah."

"That's weird."

"It *is* weird."

"Well, who the hell would do that?"

"Shit if I know," Kyle said. "Luke swears it wasn't him and, even if Keely could reach that high, I don't think she could write it out so clearly, if she could write it at all. And I know it wasn't Lisa or me." He paused for a moment, considered, then decided to go for it. "Hell, man, for a while, I thought it might be you."

"Me?"

"Yeah, you. You know the other night when we were talking about that movie?"

"What movie?" Eddie asked. "When?"

"Poker night. You were talking about that movie, *The Amityville Horror.*"

"I was?"

"Yeah, you were going 'Geettt ouuuut! Geettt ouuuut!'"

Eddie thought back for a moment, then shook his head. "No, I wasn't," he said confidently.

"Yes, you were!" Kyle insisted. "You were doing the voice and everything. 'Geettt ouuuut, geettt ouuuut!'"

"I don't remember that," Eddie said.

"Probably not," Kyle said. "We were pretty Patron'd out."

"I do remember beating your ass at poker," Eddie said.

"Of course, you remember that."

The phone rang and Eddie answered it on the second ring. "Jalama Pest Control, Eddie speaking. May I help you?"

It was Steve, one of their technicians with a question about pricing for an attic clean-out. Kyle let Eddie take the call while he meandered back to his office, soda in hand. He sat at his desk, idly checking the day's schedule, and then opened his internet browser. He searched the local newspaper first, and then the Los Angeles Times. Neither had any mention of an earthquake that morning. He expanded his search next, checking the San Francisco news website and then USA Today. Nothing there, either. Finally, he just Googled "earthquake tracking" and found a government-based website at www.earthquake.usgs.gov. He read slowly though the list of earthquakes that had been recorded that day, from all over the world, and once again discovered that there was no entry for anything in all of Ventura County.

Maybe it was just the house settling, Kyle thought, repeating the line his father always used to give him when there was an unidentified crack or rumbling at their old house in Santa Paula.

Next Kyle entered "You must leave this house now" and was stunned to discover over 383,000,000 search items listed. *No time to go through all of those,* he laughed to himself. Going back to the search box, he entered the phrase again, this time enclosing it in quotation marks. That brought up just over 134,000 hits, most of them referencing Edgar Allen Poe's *The House of Usher.* Finally, he entered the phrase in quotes and the word "chalk" at the end, which gave him only an astonishing two listings, neither of which helped him with what he was really looking for. *As if I know what I'm looking for,* Kyle thought.

The phone rang again, and Kyle answered it, hoping it was one of the technicians with a quick question. It wasn't. It was a customer from the Camarillo area, and he wasn't happy.

"I had an appointment this morning between eight and ten," buzzed the angry voice in the receiver, "And your man isn't here yet."

"I apologize for that," Kyle said, glancing at the clock on his telephone. 10:11am. "Let me get your name and number and I'll track him down for you."

"You think I have all day to sit around waiting for the bug guy?"

And so it went. The customer was fighting mad that the technician was ten minutes late, and Kyle wasn't happy about it, either. A missed appointment was one of his pet peeves. He soothed the customer as best he could and promised them someone would be there in half an hour or less. He had to offer a 10% discount, too, after the customer threatened to cancel their service and go with another company. Finally, he got the customer off the phone and punched the hang-up button, then dialed the tardy technician's cell phone number. To add insult to injury, there was no answer.

Kyle switched over to his e-mail client and dashed out a quick page to the technician, demanding a call back

ASAP. A moment after he hit the "Send" button, the phone rang again and Kyle snatched it off the cradle, certain it was the tech returning his call but cautious in case it was in fact another customer.

Instead, he was rewarded with another of those blasting, screeching bleats. He slammed the phone back into the cradle.

Screw this, he thought. *I've had enough of that shit.*

He picked up the receiver and dialed *69. Odds were the callback feature wouldn't work—it often didn't for telemarketers and calls like this—but Kyle figured it was worth the try. There were a few moments of silence, the sound of hard drives or computer chips clicking, and then the phone began to ring.

Kyle was surprised to find his pulse was racing and he felt the anticipation building in his chest. Whoever answered the phone was going to get a piece of his mind, and a stern corrective to get their goddamn phone fixed.

The phone rang three times, four, five. Kyle had just decided there was going to be no answer when there was a sterile click on the line and a familiar recorded voice began speaking:

"You've reached the residence of Kyle and Lisa Callahan," said the voice, a voice he knew, *Lisa*'s voice. "We're sorry, but we can't come to the phone at the moment, but if you leave your name and a brief message …"

There was another click, and Kyle realized that someone at the house had picked up the phone, cutting off the message. *Who the hell is that?* he wondered, *I thought everyone was at school or at work.* A split second later, a cold female voice soberly said, "You must leave this house now" and the line went dead.

Three seconds later, Kyle was burning rubber in his Toyota work truck, tearing out of the parking lot and racing toward home, only partially aware of Eddie standing near the front door of the office, staring after him with concern.

CHAPTER NINETEEN

Kyle ran the Jalama Pest Control pick-up smack over the curb and into the center of his beloved front lawn. He was out of the truck and running for the front door before the pick-up even completely stopped. His keys were in his hand, and he unlocked the door and burst inside in one fluid moment.

It had taken him all of five minutes to make the four-mile drive from the office to his home.

He rushed into the kitchen first, where the answering machine was, and was only partially surprised to find the receiver dangling from the wall phone like a possum dangling from its tail. He ran next to his bedroom, where he tore open the closet and quickly opened the gun locker, pulling out his Sig Sauer pistol and checking to be sure it was loaded.

He then began a thorough search of the house, the gun hanging in his right hand, going from room to room, peering carefully inside closets, checking doors and windows, even pulling back drapes and shower curtains. It took him almost an hour to search every inch of the house and then he started all over, once again beginning in the kitchen.

This time, he took a moment to take the receiver and put it back on the hook where it belonged. It wasn't until after he'd done so that he thought of the possibility of there being any fingerprints, but he dismissed that thought almost immediately. The odds of getting H. Farmer down here with a fingerprint kit because Kyle thought someone had answered the phone at his own home were minimal at best, humiliating at worst.

He stood in the kitchen, his eyes crawling over every little inch of space there, hunting for some clue that would tell him what had happened here, and he saw nothing. If someone had been here—and he had heard them, hadn't he?—they were long gone now, and they had done a damn fine job of cleaning up after themselves in the five minutes it took Kyle to arrive.

The phone sprang suddenly to life and its shrill electronic bells made Kyle jerk so violently that he almost pulled the trigger on the Sig Sauer, which he had all but forgotten was still clutched in his hand. He carefully set the safety on, reached over and picked up the phone.

What if it's that noise again? Kyle thought. *What if I hear that voice again?*

Slowly, he lifted the receiver and pressed the cup to his ear. He took a deep breath and said, "Hello?"

"Kyle, are you all right?" It was Lisa, and he could tell by her voice that she'd spoken to Eddie and that she was scared. "What's going on?"

"Oh, hey, honey," Kyle said, trying to sound casual. "Um, nothing. Just thought I'd come home and grab my lunch. Forgot it this morning." He couldn't bring himself to tell her about the voice he'd heard, at least not yet. They had enough to think about already. No need to add a rotten cherry to the top of a melted sundae.

"Eddie called," Lisa said. "He said you left work in a hurry. Said it seemed like something was wrong."

"I was late for an appointment," Kyle said. "I guess I forgot to mention that to him."

"You better call him," Lisa said, her concern slowly hardening into soft anger for making her worry. "He said he didn't know what the hell was going on."

"I will," he told her. "I better go now. See you tonight."

"Okay," Lisa said, somewhat dubiously. "Love you."

"Love you, too." Kyle put the phone back in the receiver and stood in the kitchen a moment, giving it one more good look around. *What the hell's going on here?* he thought. After a few moments, he pushed himself away from the counter and walked over to the fridge. Inside was the usual collection of sodas (Dr. Pepper 10 for Lisa; Coke Zero Sugar for Kyle; Sprite and Mountain Dew for the kids), staples like milk, butter and cheese, and a stack of Oscar Meyer Lunchables. An apple sitting all alone on the top shelf caught Kyle's eye, its tight, bright red skin and healthy shine made his mouth water. He grabbed that and a Coke Zero, taking pleasure in the chilly coolness of the aluminum can against his palm.

He used the tip of his boot to close the refrigerator door and, even before the door started to move, he sensed that someone was *there* and when the door swung shut and he found himself facing that person, his heart skipped a beat and his hand opened involuntarily. The Coke Zero dropped to the floor where it popped at the seam and began spraying a thin line of pressurized liquid into the air.

"Jesus!" Kyle cried and jerked as though someone had slapped him.

It was Mrs. Trellis standing there, now exposed from where she had been hidden when the refrigerator door was open.

"You scared the hell out of me," Kyle told her.

But Mrs. Trellis didn't respond. Instead, she just stood silently, her eyes softly focused in Kyle's general direction. She seemed to look *through* him rather than at him.

"Mrs. Trellis?" Kyle asked again. He waved the hand with the apple still in it in front of her face. She seemed not to notice. It was as though she was sleepwalking and, for all he knew, that's exactly what she was doing.

Kyle sat the apple on the counter and picked up the hissing Coke Zero can, tossing it gently in the sink. He turned back to his neighbor, who still hadn't moved, hadn't spoken.

"Mrs. Trellis?" Kyle said, waving his hand in front of her eyes again, feeling a cold numbness in his stomach at her lack of response. "Mrs. Trellis, are you all right?"

"You must leave this house now," Mrs. Trellis said, her eyes darting up to his, and then she collapsed into Kyle's arms.

Chapter Twenty

Lisa Callahan pulled her Toyota Camry parallel to the curb in front of her house, killed the engine and climbed out. She stood there a moment, her eyes blinking in disbelief at the bizarre scene.

Her husband's work truck was parked diagonally across the lawn. He had just missed the mailbox, pulling in at an angle that bisected the yard diagonally in almost perfect fashion. An ambulance and a police car were parked in the driveway, both currently unoccupied, the rear doors of the ambulance yawning open like a square metal cavern.

Despite the fact its occupants were elsewhere, the boxed red lights on the roof of the patrol car flashed menacingly.

Lisa was reminded of the last time she came home to find a police car sitting in her driveway. Luke had been in an accident with one of his friends, who, in his parents' absence, had decided to steal their Mercedes and their Beefeater Gin and crashed the former by hitting the latter a little too hard. Although Luke was uninjured, the police officer had decided it was a good idea to give him a ride home—and a good lecture—on the way. Luckily, especially for Luke, he had not partaken of the stolen Beefeater. Lisa remembered driving up that day and seeing the patrol car there and feeling her heart go heavy in her chest. Her first thought had been that someone had been injured or, God forbid, killed. Unlike today, she had had no advance warning about Luke's accident and, as a mother, she immediately feared the worst.

Still, even with the advance warning, Lisa felt anxious as she stepped up on the curb and started toward the house. It was so odd it almost hurt her brain to see Kyle's truck sitting in the middle of the grass, parked awkwardly like some redneck trophy car, and her concerned frown deepened when she saw the ruts the tires had dug in the turf. *Kyle loves that lawn*, she thought. *He's not going to be happy about that.* She walked around the truck, again noticing the increased gopher activity, and stepped up to the front door.

"Excuse us, miss," came a voice from the darkened doorway. Lisa halted in her tracks and then backed up. From out of the black hole of the open door came a uniformed paramedic leading a gurney out of the house. As he passed her, he gave her a brief nod and she managed a weak smile in return.

Strapped onto the gurney was Mrs. Trellis, her body gently swaying as the wheels beneath her maneuvered across the uneven cement of the front porch. Lisa looked down into the elderly woman's still face and was surprised she saw nothing. No sign of relaxed peacefulness, no trace of anger or madness. Instead, her neighbor just lay there, her well-lined face a complete blank. *She looks erased,* Lisa thought, and felt a shiver race up her spine.

Now the second paramedic, *the one in charge of the feet*, Lisa thought, cursing herself for her silliness at a time like this, came through the door and Lisa asked, "Will she be okay?"

"Hope so," the paramedic said, giving her an encouraging smile. "We'll take good care of her."

Lisa flashed him a smile of thanks that completely hid her disappointment at what she knew was a safely noncommittal answer.

A moment later, Kyle came out of the door behind them, and Lisa collapsed into him, pulling his weight against her own and reveling in the comfort she felt there.

"Your mom pick up the kids from school?" Kyle asked.

"She did," Lisa replied. "I told her we'd come get them before dinner."

Kyle nodded. "Tough day," he said.

"I guess so."

"And you don't know the half of it."

"Please don't tell me there's more," Lisa said. "I don't think my heart can stand it."

"There's more," Kyle said simply.

The door was filled again as the roundest police officer Lisa had ever seen stepped out, touching the tips of his fingers to the brim of his hat when he spotted Lisa. "You must be Mrs. Callahan," Harvey Farmer, he of the "H. Farmer" nameplate, said.

"Guilty," Lisa answered, and was immediately sorry she'd used that particular word.

"Harvey Farmer. Ventura PD."

"Thank you for coming out, officer. Is Mrs. Trellis going to be okay?"

"Hard to tell," Farmer said. "But she's in good hands. You folks try and have a nice night now. Don't worry about your neighbor. She'll be taken well care of, I can promise you that." He turned his attention to Kyle. "I believe you have my card. Call me again if you need anything."

Farmer tipped his hat again and waddled out to his squad car. It started with a muted roar and backed out of the driveway. Lisa was not surprised to see Farmer touch fingers to hat brim in farewell.

"That was a very round policeman," Lisa said.

Kyle laughed. "Yes. Very round." He gave his wife a gentle push toward the door. "Let's go inside. I have the feeling the entire neighborhood is watching us."

"You gonna move that truck?"

"It's fine where it is for now," Kyle said. "I'm too tired to even think about moving it at the moment."

They stepped into the hallway and Kyle made immediately for the refrigerator. He reached inside and pulled out a can of Dr. Pepper, which he passed over to his wife. He reached in again and came out with a can of Coke Zero, popping the can open and taking a deep swig. Lisa had tried Coke Zero, Kyle's favorite, but thought it was too sweet, preferring the taste of Dr. Pepper instead. Their fridge was perpetually stocked with both.

Lisa popped open her can, took a sip, and then sat down at the dining room table with her husband. They nursed their sodas quietly for a few moments. Lisa studied her husband's face cautiously. She could see the weariness in his eyes and in the way his mouth drooped at the corners. She was thankful that Eddie was working this coming

Saturday and not Kyle. He needed to catch up on his sleep and the weekend was the only time he had to do it.

"So, what'd the police say?" Lisa finally prompted.

"It's so freaking weird," Kyle said. "But apparently, ol' Mrs. Trellis finally lost it."

"That much is pretty obvious," Lisa said. "Why else would she be in our house in the middle of the day?"

"It's not just that," Kyle said, taking a swig of his cola. "They think she did the graffiti, too … and I didn't even tell you about the phone call."

"Phone call?"

"Yeah. Phone call," Kyle said. He told her about the screeching calls he'd been receiving, both at home and at work, and about dialing *69 to find out who had been calling. "It freaked me out enough when *our* answering machine picked up, but when some woman came on the line and told me to leave my house, I lost it. I didn't recognize Mrs. Trellis's voice. I had no idea who was in here. That's why I high-tailed it out of work."

"You told me you were late for an appointment," Lisa accused.

"I know," Kyle said. "I didn't want to scare you."

"You know, I've got those phone calls, too," Lisa confessed. "They're really annoying. It sounds like nails dragging across a chalkboard!"

Kyle snapped his fingers. "That's exactly what it is!" he said. "I've been trying to put my finger on that for days, but that's what that sound is. Nails on a chalkboard!"

"Wait a minute," Lisa said. "I was *here* when I got one of those calls. So, it couldn't have been Mrs. Trellis."

"Maybe she called from her house."

"She couldn't have. She was at the front door a split second later."

Kyle thoughtfully scratched his chin. "Well, all we know for certain is that she made at least *one* of those calls," he said. "She answered the phone *here* when I dialed star sixty-nine. As far as those other calls, maybe there really is something wrong with the phone line."

"There has to be," Lisa said. "Why would anyone call and just rake their nails across a chalkboard? If you ask me, that's a pretty boring prank call."

"Maybe," Kyle said. "But maybe not. You know that chill you get when you hear that sound?"

"I hate that. Sets my teeth on edge."

"Exactly. Maybe some jerk thinks that's funny." He paused, and a sickened look came across his face. "Maybe some jerk gets off on it."

Lisa didn't like that idea but realized that it could be a possibility. "In this day and age, there's nothing I won't believe," Lisa said. "Hold on. How do they think Mrs. Trellis reached so high to write that graffiti? She's five foot two at best!"

"Stood on a chair, stepladder, something," Kyle said. Lisa's look of disbelief was mirrored by her husband. "I know, I know," Kyle continued. "It sounded impossible to me, too. And even if she did get up there, how could she have made the letters so precise? Have you seen her hands?"

"Yes!" Lisa replied. "They shake like a leaf in the wind." She took another sip of her soda. "I'm thinking no way."

They sat and they drank, and they thought in silence. Lisa went over a list of possibilities in her mind. Was it Mrs. Trellis? Maybe. Maybe she used a ladder and maybe she used to be a schoolteacher and maybe she can still write clearly even with her palsy. Was it Keely? Not likely. She was too young to even spell correctly, much less make perfect letters. And even with the stepstool from the kitchen—which was probably too heavy for her to carry anyway—she would have had difficulty reaching up that high. Luke? Possibly. As a fifteen-year-old, he had what Kyle called "a devil inside him," a devil that raised its head when you questioned him about his homework or told him to be home early. But what reason would he have for writing "You must leave this house now" on the wall? And why would he bother? He'd much rather sit in his room, listen to that old school heavy metal his father had turned him onto, and play World of Warcraft or Star Wars Empire. Maybe Eddie Rivera? Lisa knew firsthand that Eddie could be a practical joker, but she couldn't get her mind around him breaking into their home for the sake of a joke. Someone else? Yeah, right. Who? Why? When? None of those one-word questions had anything that even closely resembled an answer.

"You know what else?" Kyle said suddenly, breaking Lisa out of her reverie. Lisa shook her head. "When I got home," Kyle continued, "I searched every room in the house top to bottom. I looked in closets, I looked behind curtains. I even opened the damned drawers and peeked inside. The doors were all locked, the windows were all closed. There was no way in or out."

"Then how'd she get in?" Lisa asked.

"That's exactly it," Kyle said. "I don't know. She wasn't there one minute and the next minute she was standing right in front of me."

"That doesn't make any sense."

"I know."

They sipped their drinks quietly, both of them turning over the chain of events in their minds and examining it from every angle. Lisa could see her husband's mind working and her own mind was a tumble of thoughts and possibilities, none of which made sense.

"There is one possibility we haven't mentioned," Lisa said, choosing her words very carefully. *Mentioned*, not *considered*. She didn't know how to continue.

"I know," Kyle said, clearing the path for her. It was as though he already knew what she was going to say.

"Maybe our house is haunted," Lisa said, and laughed nervously. But the laugh didn't ease the tension. In fact, it seemed to make it worse.

Kyle took a long swig of his Coke Zero and crumpled the can in one hand. He tossed it across the kitchen into the recycle bin in the corner.

"You know, that thought crossed my mind, too," Kyle admitted. "But that doesn't make any sense, either. We've lived her over almost six years. We've never seen any kind of ..." Lisa watched as he searched for the right word. "...*spooky* activity here in all those years. No one's been in our daughter's room in the middle of the night, no one's answered our phone when we're not home and no one's written warnings on our hallway. Houses don't suddenly *get* haunted six years after you move into them."

"Unless the father kills the entire family with a shotgun because the demons tell him they're evil."

"Yeah, but that's it for that family," Kyle said. "Then someone else moves in and the haunting begins right away. Ghosts don't wait six years to start scaring you."

They shared a nervous laugh that faded to nearly complete silence as they both contemplated. Finally, Lisa swallowed the last of her Dr. Pepper and shook her head. "Are we really sitting here, having a discussion about our house having *ghosts*?"

Kyle laughed with her. "Fucking Eddie," he said. "If he had never mentioned *The Amityville Horror*, everything would probably be just fine!"

They laughed together and Lisa felt the weight of uncertainty lift off her shoulders. It felt nice. She wanted nothing more than a quiet evening, maybe a couple of hours of mindless TV and then bed, but she still had to go pick up the kids at her mom's house, a short but necessary drive away.

She stood, snatched her keys out of the bowl on the dining room table, and announced: "I'll go get the kids."

"And I'm going to take a shower," Kyle said. He stood up and cursed suddenly, reaching down to touch his ankle. "Dammit, that thing hurts," he said.

"Is it getting any better?" Lisa asked, wincing.

"No. Not at all. Hurts like a bitch." He reached down and pulled his foot up, bending at the knee. "Do me a favor," he continued. "Would you look at it? See how it looks? Damn thing bit me in the one place I can't see." He twisted so his heel was facing up but in doing so he was forced to turn his back and look the other way.

Lisa leaned down close to the bite, the hot redness of which she could see clearly from a few feet away, and examined it closely.

It was the reddest flesh she'd ever seen in her life, swollen and hardened to a tight ball that stretched the skin to what seemed like a breaking point. Little blue lines ran out from the center to the edges and were creeping off the mound itself and onto the surrounding skin. Lisa, being married to a pest control expert, had seen many an insect bite over the years, but she'd never seen a bite so angry, so painful looking, so ready to burst. She clucked her tongue in concern.

"Oooh, honey, that looks like a bad one. Might be infected already," she said. "You better go see the doctor tomorrow."

"I may have to," Kyle said. "It hurts so bad I can barely get my socks on, much less my work boots."

"I'll call Dr. Mayner in the morning," Lisa said. "Get you an appointment."

"I've got a full day tomorrow, honey."

"Bullshit," Lisa said. "You tell Eddie you're going to the doctor tomorrow and, if he's got a problem with it, he can talk to me."

Kyle batted his eyes. "My hero," he cooed.

"Go soak that in hot water or something," Lisa said, releasing his heel and giving him a pat on the fanny. "I'll be back in ten."

She gave him a quick peck and started toward the door, stopping only long enough to take the apple that was sitting on the countertop and put it back in the refrigerator where it belonged. *They'll stay fresher that way*, Lisa remembered her mother saying, almost always followed with the old adage *An apple a day keeps the doctor away.* She allowed herself another little giggle as she stepped out onto the front porch. *An apple a day keeps the doctor away.* If Kyle had eaten that apple instead of leaving it out on the counter, maybe she wouldn't be making him a doctor's appointment.

CHAPTER TWENTY-ONE

The evening had gone pleasantly, and Kyle had to wonder if maybe the police were right. Maybe Mrs. Trellis had been the cause of all their concern. He felt a pang of sorrow for his elderly neighbor.

Lisa had returned with the kids, made sure they both bathed, ate their dinner and got to bed at the usual hours: Keely before nine and Luke at his usual 11:30-ish. The grown-ups followed them just before midnight. It had been a long, stressful day and they both slept well.

The next morning, Kyle was the first one out of bed, as usual. He showered under a hot spray, enjoying the biting mist and the morning calm, and dried off quickly. He slipped into his uniform (wincing as he put a sock and shoe over the throbbing bite), and stepped into the hallway, half expecting to see another graffiti message awaiting him. There was nothing. The morning was quiet, breaking sunny, and it looked to be a glorious day.

Kyle poured himself a bowl of Grape-Nuts, doused it with a healthy spill of milk, added a couple of teaspoons of sugar and sat at the kitchen table to eat. If it had been Lisa's breakfast, she would have let the cereal sit awhile so the tough little kernels would soften, but Kyle liked it hard and crunchy even though he knew it probably wasn't good for his teeth. Sometimes, he thought Grape-Nuts should have been called "Grape-Rocks."

He sat and enjoyed his breakfast and listened to the sounds of the rest of the house coming alive. He heard the shower in the hallway bathroom kick in and knew that Luke was up and around. He heard voices coming from his own bedroom and recognized it as that of Tom Spence and the rest of the morning team over at KVTA radio. That would be Lisa's alarm. She'd lay in bed another ten minutes, listening to Spence cracking his infamous puns, and then get up and shower. When she was done, she'd wake Keely and start getting her ready for school.

Things seemed to be back to normal.

Kyle finished his breakfast, stood, and walked over to the kitchen sink. He ran the water on the bowl, rinsing it thoroughly, making sure no individual Grape-Nut clung to the ceramic bowl. If there was one thing he hated, it was prying those little bastards off the dishware once they'd dried. They stuck to the bowl as though they were super-glued there.

He glanced out the kitchen window, marveling at what was turning out to be a beautiful day, and his shoulders slumped. There, in the middle of his lawn, sat his work truck, still parked where he had left it when he came home yesterday. *I really should have moved that*, he thought. He cocked his head as another thought registered: the truck looked as though it was sitting unevenly, its left front end lower than its right. *Dammit*, Kyle thought, *do I have a flat tire?*

He put the rinsed bowl in the wire basket, dropping his spoon into the little cup designed to hold the silverware, and dried his hands with the towel hanging on the stove handle. Then he rolled up his sleeves, unhappily anticipating the work ahead of him, and walked to the front door.

Kyle stepped out onto the porch and looked in the direction of the work truck. He froze in his tracks and his jaw dropped open in what would have been, in other circumstances, almost comical shock.

There were no flat tires on the Jalama Pest Control truck. But there were now literally *dozens* of gopher holes in the yard. It was as though the gophers had had an overnight digging party and they'd brought along their entire families to help out. The front end of the pickup sat in a grouping of holes that had collapsed, dropping the front tire into a crater the size of a trash barrel. Every square foot of the lawn was peppered with gopher holes and littered with piles of dirt. It was as though Satan had fired a shotgun up from hell and blasted a hundred holes in the Callahan's previously pristine (except for a couple of fresh tire ruts) lawn.

Kyle stood on the porch, staring in horrified awe, and realized that he had forgotten to breathe. He took a deep lungful now, shaking his head in disbelief and blinking his eyes rapidly, hoping the image before him would change. In all his years of pest control, he had never seen anything like this, especially something that happened overnight. His heart sank as he realized how much work was ahead of him. Not only did he have to get rid of the gophers, but he would also have to rebuild his entire lawn from scratch.

He finally tore his eyes away from the destruction and stepped back into the house. Lisa was just heading down the hallway toward Keely's room, tying her morning robe around her, and Kyle ran over and stopped her. "You gotta see this," he said. He tugged on the sleeve of her robe, and she followed him to the front door.

Kyle took her out onto the porch and waved his arm like a presenter at a game show. Lisa followed the direction of his wave and Kyle watched as her face transformed from a look of puzzled curiosity to a grimace of total horror. She reached out and grabbed his shoulder for support.

"Jesus *Christ*, Kyle. What the hell happened?"

Kyle shook his head. "All I can tell you…" he said. "…is that Mrs. Trellis didn't do this."

Chapter Twenty-Two

Lisa was scheduled for the breakfast shift that day so, after dropping the kids off at school, she headed directly to Souper Salad World. She sat in the parking lot for a moment, calling Dr. Mayner's office and setting an appointment for Kyle that afternoon. The receptionist tried to tell her that the earliest appointment available was late next week, but Lisa wouldn't have it, telling the receptionist that her husband was in great pain and needed to see the doctor today. After some minor grumbling, the receptionist said she might be able to "fit him in" at 3:15 and Lisa thanked her and hung up. She then sent Kyle a quick text about the appointment.

As usual, the breakfast rush was busy, mostly with senior citizens who lived in the area, but also a few commuters or salespeople with time on their hands and, of course, the occasional family, whom Lisa always assumed had to be on vacation. Otherwise, who had time to bring the entire family to breakfast on a weekday?

Things went well with no major complaints, except for one jerk who insisted that pizza should be served at every meal because it was featured in their television ads. Lisa placated him with a Free Lunch coupon (which she was certain was the creep's goal in the first place).

It was just after 11 when she got her first break. "I'll be right back," she told Brenda, "Got to make a phone call." Brenda gave her the A-OK sign and Lisa stepped out to the Camry.

There wasn't really any office space (except for Cal Rosen's cluttered mess) or a break room at Souper Salad Bar so Lisa often took her breaks in her car. Sometimes she'd grab a little snack from the dessert table and other times she'd just sit there for fifteen or twenty minutes, reading a book (that's where she'd read all of *Fifty Shades of*

Grey, where no one else could see her) or listening to the radio (usually the local pop station with its Lady Gagas, Katy Perrys and Miley Cyruses).

Today, however, she picked up her cellphone and called Gina, hoping her friend was on break as well or at least somewhere she could talk.

"What's up, girlfriend?" Gina answered on the third ring.

"Hey," Lisa said. "Got a few minutes to talk?"

"Sure!" Gina said. "Let me just finish up at this house and I'll go back to the truck, then we can talk all we want."

Lisa waited quietly while her friend completed her delivery and went back to her vehicle. She often envied Gina and her job with the Post Office. She got out in the sun, she got to meet a lot of people—whom she would come to know well after delivering their mail year after year— and she was well paid. Of course, there was the bad side, too: Delivering mail in the rain and cold, the stress on your back from carrying large bags, and dealing with the assholes of the world who would bitch and complain no matter how well you did your job.

Oh, Lisa knew those people well! She'd just given one a Free Lunch coupon!

After a moment, Gina came back on the line. "All right. So, what's up?"

"This is gonna be weird," Lisa said. "But stay with me."

"Yay! I love weird!"

"Well, you know all those troubles we've been having at home …" and Lisa went on to explain all about the woman in her daughter's room, the writing on the wall, finding the catatonic Mrs. Trellis in the kitchen. She told her about her nightmares, about the gopher destruction. She told her about the screeching calls and how at least some of them had come from their home phone number. She told her everything she could remember about the past few days and, as she unloaded, she was disturbed to find that, instead of feeling better about it all by getting it off her chest, she felt worse! Lumped together all there in one conversation, Lisa realized that it all sounded crazy!

"So that policeman told you that your neighbor, Mrs. Trellis…?"

"Yes, Mrs. Trellis."

"So, he told you that Mrs. Trellis did all that stuff?"

"Well, not all of it, of course. Mrs. Trellis didn't train gophers to chew up our lawn."

"Yeah, I know that. But I mean, he said she did the writing, she broke into your home, she made all those phone calls?"

"Yeah," Lisa said, her voice dripping sarcasm. "That 90-year-old, five-foot woman did all that. That's what he thinks."

"That policeman is *high!*" Gina spat. "He's probably been smoking some of that high power weed they have locked up in the evidence room!"

That gave Lisa a little smile.

"You know what it sounds like to me?" Gina said soberly. "It sounds like what I told you earlier. I think your place is haunted."

Lisa felt her breath catch in her throat, hesitated, then said, "Gina, seriously ..."

"I am serious!" Gina insisted. "I watch enough *Paranormal Activity* and *Ghost Hunters* to know that ghosts don't look like *Casper*. They *do* stuff, like write on the walls, show up in the middle of the night, and make animals do their bidding. I'm telling you, Lisa, does any of that sound familiar?"

Lisa had to admit that it did. "So, what do I do?" she asked. "I mean, just for the sake of argument, let's say it *is* a ghost. What do I do?"

"Depends," Gina told her. "Maybe that ghost is trying to tell you something. Maybe someone was murdered in that house years before you bought it and their bones are hidden there. Maybe they want you to find them so they can finally rest in peace! Maybe they just don't want you in their house, think it's theirs, not yours."

"Or maybe our house is built on an ancient Indian burial ground," Lisa said jokingly.

"Maybe something like that!" Gina exclaimed.

"Okay," Lisa said again. "But the question remains: What do we do?"

Gina was uncharacteristically quiet for a moment. Then she said: "You need to find out more about your house. You need to do some research."

"You mean, like on the internet?"

"Well, maybe a little of that," Gina said. "But I'm talking more of a *local* history. You need to find out who owned your house before you did, what happened there before you moved in, what your house is built on. Anything that might be waking this ghost up."

"Okay, but we've lived there almost *six years*," Lisa said. "Why now?"

"No one except your ghost knows that," Gina said. "You know, there's this guy. Lives here in Ventura. Works for the city, I think, in the downtown museums. He's a famous historian for the area and he also dabbles in supernatural stuff."

"Chambers," Lisa said. "Eric Chambers."

"That's him!"

"Yeah, I read about him a lot in the newspaper, especially at Halloween time. He does tours or something."

"Yeah, ghost tours! You should talk to him. If anything weird happened in your house, he'll know about it. He'll probably know if your house is built on a pet cemetery …"

"…or an Indian burial ground," Lisa said again.

"...or an Indian burial ground," Gina agreed. "That's who you want to talk to. That's what I'd do. I'd call Eric Chambers. Have him come out and take a look."

"Can't hurt," Lisa said. "Maybe I'll give him a call."

"I would," Gina said firmly. "I would."

"Okay, Gina. Thanks for your help."

"You're welcome and you know it!" Gina said.

"I know it," Lisa said. "But there is one thing..."

"Yes?"

"Has anybody ever told you that you probably watch too many movies?"

They shared a laugh and said goodbye.

Lisa glanced at her watch. Ten minutes remained on her break. She leaned back in the comfortable cloth seat and let the thoughts roll through her mind. The fact of the matter was that the case had already been solved: The dementia suffering Mrs. Trellis was the culprit for at least housebreaking and probably for the phone calls and the writing on the wall of the hallway. Everything else could be explained away as bad luck or coincidence.

Or could it?

For example, who *was* that woman who had been standing at the foot of Keely's bed? Lisa was sure she'd really seen her, as sure now as she'd been at the time. Even though the other three family members in the room had seen nothing, Lisa could still visualize the woman's deep black hair, pulled back in what looked like an uncomfortable bun, and her crisp, conservative black dress with its doily-like collar.

It seemed silly to start calling a ghost hunter, based on what they'd seen so far. And Lisa was fairly certain that, if there had been any bones to be found at the house on Neath Street, they would have found them already. They'd lived there for almost six years, after all. And she was practically 100% sure the house hadn't been built on top of a pet cemetery or Native American burial ground.

Plus, Kyle had been right: No house suddenly *becomes* haunted after a family has lived there peacefully for over half a decade.

That's it, she decided, *I'm going to forget about Eric Chambers unless something else happens. Something a little more substantial, like the walls bleeding or a severed head floating around the room moaning about his lost ribcage.*

Lisa glanced at the dash clock again and realized her break was over in four minutes. She tucked her cellphone back into her purse and had just opened the car door when the phone rang, the strains of Elton John's "The Bitch is Back" announcing that Gina was calling again.

"Speak fast," Lisa answered playfully. "I've got to get back to work."

"Don't bother calling Eric Chambers," Gina said.

"Funny you should say that. I was just thinking …"

"Because I called him for you!" Gina announced. "He's going to meet us after work for drinks. At The Cave. Six o'clock. See you then!"

And she was gone before Lisa could ask even one of the myriad questions that suddenly popped into her mind, including *Are you kidding?*

A few seconds later, however, Lisa shrugged, telling herself, *What would be the harm?* And, anyway, a glass of wine (or two) after work didn't seem like a bad idea.

CHAPTER TWENTY-THREE

Kyle arrived at Dr. Mayner's office at 2:45pm, checked in, and sat down in the waiting room for what he knew would probably be a long haul. Even though his appointment was scheduled for 3:15, he didn't expect to be called in to see the doctor until closer to four. That had been his experience ever since he started going to Dr. Mayner a dozen years earlier, but he thought it was a fair trade-off for the excellent attention and care his family received. Plus, it gave him a chance to read some of his book.

Kyle loved to read but very rarely got the opportunity. Work was the first hurdle. At almost 60 hours a week, Kyle often had very little time for anything except working, resting, and then going to work again. And then there were the other things that got in the way: household chores, family commitments and, of course (he laughed silently), poker night with the Riveras.

Kyle settled back, opened his book (it was Stephen King's *Dr. Sleep*) and allowed himself to be absorbed.

Twenty minutes later, the nurse had to call his name twice before Kyle could be pulled out of the new adventures of Danny Torrance. He apologized, marked his place with the McDonald's receipt serving as a bookmarker, and followed the nurse into the back room. She quickly weighed him (Kyle's least favorite part of any doctor visit), took his blood pressure and guided him to a small patient room and a chair there.

"The doctor will be right with you," the nurse said, and closed the door. Kyle quickly translated from nurse-speak to English: "The doctor will be with you in about ten minutes."

As they tended to do when in an examination room, Kyle's eyes quickly scanned the sink and counter and, as always, he was privately delighted when he found the wooden sticks they placed on your tongue when you went "ahhhhhh." Those sticks held so many memories that it gave him some inexplicable pleasure in seeing them there. Content with his discovery and smiling like a schoolchild as some of those memories flooded past, Kyle opened his book again.

Almost exactly ten minutes later, Dr. Mayner arrived. Kyle knew this because he could hear the doctor scrabbling for the clipboard hung on the other side of the door. As Mayner entered, Kyle once again found himself staring in awe at Mayner's fur-covered face. The man had the bushiest beard Kyle had ever seen, not long, just bushy, and it seemed to crawl out of his collar and onto his face like some sort of furry parasite. On anyone else, it would have looked ridiculous (*like those guys on* Duck Dynasty, Kyle thought) but Mayner pulled it off with surprising class and dignity.

"Hello, doctor," Kyle took Mayner's extended hand and shook it.

"Good to see you, Kyle," Mayner said. "How are things?"

"Not too bad," Kyle said. "Well, except for this damn bite."

"Yes, let's take a look at that," Mayner said. He patted the paper-sheeted exam bed. "Have a seat there for a minute, please." He waited while Kyle removed his sock and boot. "How're Lisa and the kids?"

"Doing well, thanks. Everybody's doing well." *The neighbor, not so much,* Kyle thought with a guilty inward smile.

Dr. Mayner dropped to his knees and peered briefly at the back of Kyle's ankle. "Yeah, that doesn't look good," he said. "Hard to get at from this angle. Do me a favor, roll over and lay on your stomach. Dangle your feet off the edge here."

Kyle did as told, rolling over onto his stomach and lying flat on the exam bed, the paper sheet crinkling noisily beneath him, while Dr. Mayner got a closer look at his foot. After a moment, Dr. Mayner asked, "And how'd you say this happened?"

"Not sure," Kyle said. "I first noticed it at a bed bug service, figured I got bit there. But it could have happened a few hours before I guess."

"Does it hurt?" Mayner asked.

"Yeah, it hurts," Kyle said, thinking *Duh!* "I have a hard time putting my shoes on, it hurts so much."

Mayner examined the bite for a few more moments, then said, "Well, here's the thing: this is no bite."

"It's not a bite?"

"No. It's more of … it's closer to a cyst."

"You mean, like cancer?" Kyle said, feeling his blood go cold.

"No, probably not cancer," Mayner clarified. "I'm thinking it's probably filled a fluid of some kind. When did you say your first noticed this?"

"Two days ago."

"And there was nothing there before?"

"No. Nothing."

"Then probably not cancer." Mayner sat quietly a moment, gently poking and prodding at the bite. "It wouldn't have grown this big in just two days." He considered the swollen ankle briefly, then stood and walked around to the head of the bed so he could talk to Kyle more comfortably. "Okay," he said, "Here's the thing: I can send you to a specialist who will look at this, examine it from every angle, and then lance it and drain it. But that'll take a week or so. You're not going to get an appointment right away and I know this hurts."

"It does," Kyle said.

"Or," Mayner continued. "I can lance it here. Odds are it's just a cyst filled with blood or pus, and I can lance it, drain it, give you a fistful of anti-biotics and send you on your way."

"What if it's not?" Kyle asked.

"What if it's not a cyst?" Mayner said. "First, I'm 90% certain that it is. Second, we can always send you off to that specialist."

"What would you recommend?" Kyle asked.

"Six of one, half a dozen of the other," Mayner said. "I'm sure you're anxious to get back on your feet without hurting. I believe this will do it … or at least get you going in that direction."

Kyle shrugged, not an easy task while lying face down on an exam table. "Well, I say let's do it," he said. "The sooner we can pop that thing, the better."

"Very good," said Mayner. "Let me get Sherry in here to get you prepped. Shouldn't take long."

Kyle waited yet another ten minutes, bored now that he couldn't reach his book on the table behind him, while Sherry buzzed in and out of the exam room, bringing supplies and tools, some of which Kyle didn't like the sight of at all. There was the stainless-steel lancet, which looked more like a tool for working on leather than for piercing human skin, and the scalpel, whose shiny silver surface only emphasized the razor-sharp edge of its blade. There was also a small hypodermic needle, but that bothered Kyle the least. He had never been bothered by needles.

I hope he's got some serious anesthetic, Kyle thought. *Those things look like they're gonna hurt like a bitch.*

"I don't think you'll need any anesthetic," Mayner said upon his return, squeezing his hands into rubber gloves and snapping them just like a TV doctor. "Just a little topical. But this might pinch a bit."

Kyle didn't believe him for a minute. Doctors always said you were going to feel a "pinch" and that pinch always hurt like hell. He thought about asking for anesthetic anyway but didn't want to sound like a pussy. He decided to stick it out, no matter how much it hurt. And, really, how painful could it be?

He thought back to putting his shoes and socks on this morning and realized the answer was *Very*.

"All right, we're going to try lancing it first," Mayner said. "Let me know if this is too painful."

Kyle clamped down his teeth and prepared himself for the pain. Sherry put her hand on his and patted gently. The cyst hurt plenty as Mayner touched and prodded it, trying to locate the best lancing position, and Kyle braced himself for the puncture. He was rather surprised, and hugely grateful, when Dr. Mayner announced: "Okay, we're in. Now let's see what's hiding in here."

A few moments of maddening silence passed. Then, Mayner said simply: "Hmmmm."

What does that mean? Kyle thought. He wanted desperately to ask but was loathe to interrupt Mayner's thought process.

"Nothing," Mayner said finally. "Let me try another angle."

And the poking and prodding began again. This time, Kyle did feel that promised little pinch when the lancet slid in … but only a little one.

There were a few more moments of silence and then another "Hmmm" from Dr. Mayner.

Kyle couldn't stop himself. "Any luck?"

Mayner hesitated a moment, and Kyle got the feeling he was thinking over his words carefully. "So, here's the thing," Mayner said. "There is apparently no fluid inside this cyst, or whatever it is, so there's nothing to drain. If you're all right with it, Kyle, I'd like to open it up a little, take a look inside."

"That sounds painful," Kyle said quietly.

"Well, yes," Dr. Mayner said, "But I'll give you a local anesthesia for the pain. If this doesn't tell us anything, then we'll send you off to that specialist."

I don't want to do this, Kyle thought. "Let's do it," he said aloud.

"Very well," said Dr. Mayner. He dropped the useless lancet on the stainless-steel tray and picked up the hypodermic needle. "You're going to feel a little pinch," he said again, and plunged the needle home. Kyle felt a little pinch, all right. For a second, his skin lit up like it was on fire but a second later it was gone, followed by a cool, blue numbness.

"We'll let that take for a few seconds," Mayner said. "Once we're finished here, we'll wash out the wound very carefully, pack it up with some medicine and bandages, and send you on your way. It should heal very quickly, as long as you take it easy. Hopefully, we won't need any stitches, but it depends on how deep I have to dig."

I really wish you hadn't said that, Kyle thought. *"How deep I have to dig" is not a phrase you want to hear from your doctor.*

"All right, let's give this a shot," Mayner said.

I could use a shot right about now, Kyle thought. *Of tequila!*

Sherry started the hand-patting again as Kyle waited for the slashing burn of the incision. But it never came. *That's some pretty good local anesthetic,* he thought. But his positive critique of the anesthetic was forgotten when Sherry suddenly gasped, and the hand-patting came to a sudden halt. A split second later, Dr. Mayner heightened the tension with an under-the-breath "What the hell?"

Kyle winced. "What is it?" he asked nervously. "Doctor? What is it?"

He felt Mayner stop digging on the wound and waited what seemed an eternity as the doctor came around the bed to stand in front of him. Kyle looked up expectantly and Mayner obliged, putting his latex-gloved hand down, palm up, and opening his fingers.

There, in the middle of the doctor's palm, was a crumbling stack of tiny red worms, wiry and thin, not moving but curling around each other as if holding on in a death grip. Kyle had a flash image of blood-red shredded wheat and couldn't stop himself from bleating "What the hell is that?"

Dr. Mayner was quiet for what seemed a full minute, as Kyle stared in terror at the hideous mess in the doctor's hand. Finally, the doctor took a deep breath, shook his head slowly, eyebrows raised, and announced:

"That appears to be rubber eraser rubbings," he said. "That's what the hell that is."

CHAPTER TWENTY-FOUR

The digital watch on Kyle Callahan's left wrist read 4:55pm. He'd been in Dr. Mayner's office for just over two hours now. That was the bad news. The better news was that the good doctor had cleaned out the wound, removed every trace of whatever substance the cyst had been packed with (Kyle had a hard time believing it was *rubber eraser dust*, for Christ's sake) and patched him up. "You won't need any stitches," Mayner had told him, "I closed it up with some butterfly bandages and that should be enough. But go easy on it, try to stay off your feet as much as possible. And if you see any bleeding or if it swells like that again, give me a call and we'll get you back in here."

Kyle had to admit his foot felt better already. Although it was sore where Dr. Mayner had been working on it, the pain was nothing compared to what it had been earlier. And the hot swelling that had threatened to burst the skin there was gone completely. In fact, everything practically felt like new.

Plus, it was going to give him an office day. A chance to catch up on paperwork! *Sorry, Eddie*, Kyle thought, *but you're going to have to take care of any problems in the field. I'm supposed to stay off my feet!*

Sherry returned to the exam room a moment later with a prescription slip and a business card. "Get this prescription on your way home," she instructed. "You'll need to start taking these antibiotics tonight. And here's Dr. Mayner's card should you experience any pain, swelling or other issues. It's his service, but they'll get hold of him."

"Thanks," Kyle told her. Sherry gave him a smile and held the exam room door open. Kyle stood wearily and cautiously, assessing the pain in his heel before putting all his weight on the foot. He was happily surprised to see that there was virtually no pain. "So, that was weird," he said, watching Sherry's face as she nodded in agreement. "You ever see anything like that before?"

Sherry shook her head again. "Nope," she said simply. "Not even close."

Kyle walked out toward the waiting room, passing Dr. Mayner, busy at his desk, scribbling away on some sort of notepad. *Probably writing about the previously undiscovered Rubber Eraser Heel for the New England Journal of Medicine.* "Thanks again, doctor," Kyle said.

"Good night, Kyle," Mayner said. "Say hello to the family."

"Will do."

Kyle had just arrived at his work truck when his cell-phone buzzed in his shirt pocket. He snatched it out, switching it from *Vibrate* to *Ring* and answered, "Kyle Callahan."

"Honey, where are you?" It was Lisa, and Kyle realized he hadn't spoken to her since this morning.

"Just leaving the doctor's office," Kyle said. "On my way home."

"How'd it go?" Lisa asked.

Kyle laughed. "It went *weird*," he said. "But it's all good now. I'll tell you all about it when I get home."

"Well, I won't be home until about eight or so," Lisa said. "I'm meeting Gina for drinks."

"Tonight?" Kyle asked, checking his mental calendar to see if it was off a day or two. "Aren't we on for poker?"

"We decided to re-schedule," Lisa said, and Kyle knew by "we" she meant Lisa and Gina. "I won't be long, just one drink. Then I'll be home. Maybe I'll bring In-N-Out."

"Sounds good," Kyle said.

"What'd the doctor say?"

"Trust me," Kyle said. "It'll wait till you get home."

"That's right, keep me guessing," Lisa said. "Luke will keep an eye on Keely until you get here."

"Okay," Kyle said. "I'll be home in ten minutes or so."

"See you tonight," Lisa said. "Love you."

"Love you, too," Kyle replied, and ended the call.

He climbed in the cab, started the engine and headed for home.

CHAPTER TWENTY-FIVE

It's almost déjà vu, Lisa Callahan thought as she walked through the bottle store of the Ventura Wine Company and toward the bar area of The Cave, the restaurant located therein. Once again, there sat Gina at the bar, her purse hanging on a hook beneath the counter, a stemless glass brimming with white wine before her. She brightened and gave Lisa a little wave as she walked in.

"What's up, girl?" Gina said excitedly. A little too excitedly, Lisa thought. *She should get out more often.* "Wine?"

"Just one," Lisa said, holding up a single finger. "Those two Mai Tais we had last time got me drunk and almost pregnant." She sat down beside Gina and opened her purse, withdrew her wallet and started thumbing through compartments. "What are you drinking?" she asked.

"Calera Chardonnay," Gina responded. "And it is mmm mmm good!"

A server approached them. She was a pretty, petite woman whom Lisa thought looked much too young to vote, much less serve wine.

"Hi," she said, giving Lisa an effervescent smile. "What can I get you?"

Lisa nodded at Gina's glass. "I'll have what she's having," she said.

"You won't be sorry," Gina told her.

"I'll be right back," said the server.

Before they knew it, the young woman returned with a glass of golden liquid. Lisa thanked her and took a sip.

"Well?" Gina asked upon Lisa's return.

"You bet," Lisa said. She took a sip of her wine. Delicious. Fruity enough, but not too sweet.

"It's my favorite, I think," Gina snickered. "This is my second one!"

"You've had two already?" Lisa asked.

"You wouldn't believe how much better Eddie looks after two," Gina laughed. "Or more!"

"That's not nice," Lisa playfully scolded. She took another pull on her wine, looked around the nearly empty bar, and asked, "Okay, where's your ghost hunter?"

"He'll be here," Gina said. "He said six o'clock. It's seven minutes to!"

"I'm not sure about this," Lisa said. "We're probably making way more out of it than we need to."

"Maybe," Gina agreed. "But maybe not. You got to admit, baby doll, there's been some weird shit going down at your place."

"Weird, maybe," Lisa said. "But supernatural? I'm not buying it."

"Well, why don't we let the expert decide," Gina said. "He just walked in." She stood and waved at a gentleman making his way through the wine store toward them. "Mr. Chambers? Over here?"

Lisa turned and got her first look at Eric Chambers, ghost hunter. She'd read about him in the newspaper, seen his class descriptions in the college class catalogs, but she'd never seen him in person, couldn't even remember seeing a photograph of him for that matter. She was at once surprised and not surprised by what she saw.

He looks like a cross between the Phantom of the Opera and an old-school newspaper reporter, Lisa thought, as she watched Chambers close the gap between them. He was wearing a dusty black suit, several years out of style and as plain as it could be, along with an equally dusty black fedora and a gray scarf wrapped loosely around his throat. A pair of thin-rimmed eyeglasses sat on his nose, their perfect circles perched directly over the center of his eyes. *John Lennon glasses,* Lisa thought, *or maybe John Denver.* Chambers wore a close-cut beard that looked like a spraying of steel wool across his jawline. And he was removing a pair of gloves. *Driving gloves,* Lisa thought, as Chambers approached the two women.

Lisa guessed he was about fifty years old, but she realized that his clothes style and the gray hair that fell to just above his shoulders might be telling another story. He might be a little younger, he might be a little older, but she guessed she was in the ballpark.

"Mrs. Callahan?" Chambers asked, reaching to take Gina's out-stretched hand.

"Actually, Mr. Chambers, I'm Gina, Gina Rivera," Gina said. "I spoke to you on the phone today, but I was calling for my friend here, Lisa Callahan."

Now it was Lisa's turn to shake Chambers' hand. "Nice to meet you, Mr. Chambers," Lisa said.

"A pleasure, Mrs. Callahan," Chambers said. And Lisa thought he gave her the slightest bow.

"Please call me Lisa," Lisa said.

"Only if you agree to call me Eric," Chambers said.

"It's a deal," Lisa agreed.

"Then I'm Gina," Gina said. "Shall we get a table?"

"That would probably be best," Chambers said. "Let me get those for you."

Chambers took the two glasses of wine and carried them into The Cave. He chose a corner booth, where there were comfortable sofas and a low table and set down their wine glasses.

They sat, Lisa and Gina on one side and Chambers on the other. He neatly folded his gloves, dropped them on the table and pulled a small ringed notepad out of his coat pocket.

"What kind of wine do you like?" Gina asked.

"Merlot, if they have it," Chambers said.

"Oh, they have it," Gina confirmed, and waved down the server.

As they waited to give Chambers' order, Lisa sipped her wine and thought about how weird all this was. Here she was, a nearly 40-year-old woman, sitting at a wine bar with her best friend and a relative stranger to discuss the possible haunting of the home she'd shared with her husband and children for the past five-plus years.

Surreal.

The server returned a few moments later with a brimming glass of dark red wine. Chambers took a sip of his merlot, made an appreciative face and said, "Thank you for inviting me here tonight, ladies. I've had a long week at the museum, regaling tourists with exotic tales of what Ventura used to be."

"*Was* it exotic?" Gina asked.

"Not at all," Chambers answered. "But it was utterly fascinating. And still is. Have either of you been to the museum?"

Lisa and Gina gave each other a glance, and then both shook their heads guiltily.

"Don't feel bad," Chambers said. "Most of the locals *don't* go to the museum. Much like the inhabitants of New York, or probably any other town for that matter, we locals assume that interesting attractions like the museum are always going to be there, and that we'll visit them another day. Only that other day never seems to come."

Chambers gave a little smile that said, "But that's the way it is," and held his glass high. "Here's to Ventura," he toasted. "City by the Sea."

They clinked their glasses, and each had a sip. Chambers opened his notepad and pulled out a pen. Lisa wasn't surprised to discover it was a fountain tip. "So, your friend here tells me you have a ghost," Chambers said flatly.

Lisa felt herself blush. "Oh, no, no," she said. "I never said that. It's *not* a ghost."

Chambers eyed her curiously and Lisa realized he was silently asking, *Then what am I doing here?*

"Well, *something's* been going on at my house," Lisa added quickly. "And some of the things we can't explain."

"Tell me about it," Chambers said.

"Well, I don't really know where to start," Lisa said. She shot Gina a piercing look that said *I told you this wasn't a good idea.*

"How about starting with the address," Chambers said.

"Oh," Lisa said. "It's 127 Neath Street, in Ventura."

Chambers quickly jotted that down in his notebook. "Single floor or multi-story?" he asked.

"Single floor," Lisa asked.

"Attic or cellar?"

"Attic," Lisa confirmed, "No cellar."

"And what kind of hauntings have you experienced?" Chambers asked, sitting back and looking her in the eyes. Lisa was taken somewhat aback by his straight-forward nature. He might as well have been asking her what color her curtains were.

Lisa hesitated, taking a deep breath and weighing her options. She could call this whole thing off right now, save face and offer to buy Chambers another drink in apology for wasting his time. Or she could just tell him what she knew and see what he thought of it. See what conclusions the expert would make. Maybe he'd just tell her she was one crazy mother. And, really, at this point, what was the harm in that?

So, she told him. Everything from the mysterious, disappearing bed bugs to the discovery of Mrs. Trellis in their home. As she spoke, he nodded and jotted down notes in a quick but sharply legible fashion. At one point, he asked her to pause while he removed his hat, revealing a sparse head of graying hair on top, and caught up with his notes.

By the time she was finished, Chambers had filled over ten pages of the small notepad with his laser-precise handwriting. He closed the notebook, tucked it into his coat pocket, and finished off his merlot.

"Another?" Chambers asked, wiggling his empty glass.

"Of course," Gina said quickly. Lisa shook her head, no.

"You two go ahead," she said.

"You're no fun, girl," Gina said, poking Lisa's leg playfully beneath the table.

"Saving it for Tuesday," Lisa told her. "Tuesday is Girls' Night Out," she explained to Chambers.

Lisa waited patiently while her friend and their guest had their glasses re-filled. Chambers took another appreciative sip and asked, "How long have you two been friends?"

"Six years now," Gina said.

"And have you witnessed any of these bizarre happenings at the Callahan home?" Chambers asked Gina.

"Um, no," Gina admitted. "But if Lisa says they happened, they happened."

"Oh, I'm not doubting Lisa for a moment," Chambers said, as a server suddenly appeared with three glasses of water.

"I asked for it," Lisa said on Gina's questioning look. "Thanks," she told the server.

"Of course," the server replied, taking their empties and moving away.

"As I was saying, I'm not doubting Lisa for a moment," Chambers continued. "In fact, I tend to believe every word." He turned his attention fully to Lisa. "The events you've described are a near textbook case of a true haunting."

Lisa felt her body temperature drop. She felt dizzy and again found it impossible to believe she was actually having *this* conversation … and getting *this* response.

"What … what do you mean?" she asked.

"A true haunting isn't what you see in the movies," Chambers told her. "It's not skeletons bursting out of the floor or transparent people floating down hallways." He smiled mirthfully. "Well, it *usually* isn't."

"What is it then?" asked Gina.

"It's more of a nuisance," Chambers said. "True ghosts are more annoying than they are terrifying. They rattle cabinets, they close doors, they vibrate dishes. They cry and they wail, and they drive you nuts when you're trying to sleep. I've even seen photos of written messages …"

Lisa felt her heart stop.

"… but only on mirrors and usually when the intended recipient is stepping out of a hot shower."

"Not on hallway walls," Lisa breathed.

"Not usually," Chambers said. "But the concept is the same."

It was quiet for a moment, and Lisa found herself wishing she'd had another glass of wine after all.

"The key here is that they won't hurt you," Chambers said. "They're just left-over energy. Someone has left the world in a violent way, either by the hand of someone else or their own. And not just physical violence, but mental or psychological violence. The energy created by such an incredibly traumatic exit leaves behind unspent energy in this world, which we interpret as ghosts and hauntings. But they have no real physical presence and thus can't inflict any pain or injury." Chambers opened his hands, palms up. "Nobody hurt at your house, right?"

Lisa nodded. "Right," she said.

"And nobody will be," Chambers replied. "Unless …"

Lisa's blood froze again. "Unless what?"

"You mentioned that you have a young girl at home. How old is she?"

"Keely is almost six."

"Pre-pubescent," Chambers said matter-of-factly.

"*I beg your pardon?*" Gina said. Lisa could feel the anger behind the question.

"I'm sorry for the indelicacy," Chambers explained. "But there have been reported instances of poltergeist activity that have actually been the work of leftover energy from pubescent girls, rather than departed spirits. In those cases, however, the situation tends to get a bit more ... violent."

"Violent?" Lisa spat.

"I'm afraid so," Chambers said. "To the best of my knowledge, no one has been killed, but there have been reports of scratches and bruises, as well as broken furniture and even fires."

"Holy shit," Gina said.

"But I believe your daughter is too young," Chambers said. "Plus, from what you've told me, she's actually the least affected by this entire situation."

"That's true," Lisa said. "Actually, both of the kids seem to be kind of ignoring this stuff."

"That is curious indeed," Chambers said. "As is the fact that you haven't noticed any activity until just a few months ago," Chambers said. "I've never heard of a house suddenly becoming haunted after six years … except, of course, in those poltergeist situations I just mentioned."

"So, what do we do?" Lisa asked.

"First I'd like to do a walk-through with a psychic friend of mine," Chambers said. "Maybe she can contact the spirit or spirits at work here and find out what they seek. Are you available tomorrow afternoon, Mrs. Callahan? Say, 2pm?"

Rosen had scheduled her for the Saturday lunch shift. *Screw it*, Lisa thought. *I'll call in sick.*

"Yes, I can be there."

"Splendid. We'll meet at your home, then."

"And what if you can't contact the spirit?"

"Well, either way, I'm going to hit the books, do a little research. The area where your home is now located wasn't always a housing tract. There were homes there, of course, but there were other things as well. A public swimming pool, for one, if I remember correctly. I'll look into the history of your area and see if I can't find something we can use."

"And what do we do once you figure that out?" Lisa asked.

"*If* we figure that out," Chambers said. He shrugged his shoulders. "We won't know until we come to that."

"But you're sure we're in no danger?" Lisa asked.

"I'm quite positive," Chambers said. "The only recorded incidents of injuries from true hauntings were from minor accidents: Someone walking into the edge of a door that wasn't open before, a slip on a pool of water that suddenly appeared out of nowhere and, of course, countless hours of lost sleep from noisy spirits."

"So, it's not like the movies?" Gina asked.

"It is most definitely not like the movies," Chambers confirmed.

"What's the worst-case scenario?" Lisa said.

"Worst-case scenario?" Chambers repeated. "Worst case scenario is that you *move*," he told her.

Lisa suddenly felt her face flush and the boil of anger rose up inside of her. "That's our home," she said evenly. "We are *not* moving."

"I'm sure it won't come to that," Chambers said.

Lisa nodded again, then reached over and grabbed Gina's chardonnay. Gina didn't even protest as Lisa took a mighty pull.

"So, how many ghosts have you actually seen?" Gina asked Chambers.

Chambers gave a wry laugh. "None," he said, to the women's surprise. "That's why I hunt them. They have always fascinated me, ever since I was a little boy, but I have never had the opportunity to see one in the wild." He laughed briefly at his choice of words and took another sip of his merlot. "That's why I do this. Because, one day, I hope to do so."

Eric Chambers had no idea that, in less than 24 hours, he would be realizing his life-long dream.

CHAPTER TWENTY-SIX

Kyle Callahan was tilted back comfortably in his La-Z-Boy chair, his feet propped on the built-in ottoman. A half-empty can of MadeWest Brewing Company's Hazy IPA sat on the end table beside him, alongside a pint glass containing the other half of the beer. He was watching last week's episode of *Westworld,* a show that he loved but couldn't get Lisa to watch because, in her words, it "didn't make a damn bit of sense."

He heard keys in a lock and the laundry room door peeled open. A few seconds later, Lisa entered the living room, carrying a cardboard tray, the contents of which filled the room with a savory, mouth-watering aroma. *In-N-Out*, Kyle thought. *That's what a hamburger's all about! Yeah, baby!*

"Hi, honey," Lisa said, handing the tray to Kyle.

"Hey, baby," Kyle said. He lifted the box to his nose and sniffed deeply. If there was such a thing as an olfactory orgasm, Kyle thought he might be having one.

"Where are the kids?" Lisa asked, taking off her coat.

"Luke's staying the night over at Bradshaw's," Kyle told her. "Keely's in her room, playing with her Monster Magnet dolls."

"Monster *High*," Lisa corrected. "Monster Magnet is a band."

"I'll take Monster Magnet any day,"

"Of course, you would," Lisa said. "I'm gonna go change. Back in a minute."

"I'm probably going to start without you," Kyle said, holding the cardboard tray up.

"I know you are," Lisa said. "I'd expect nothing less."

Kyle stepped into the kitchen and took three paper plates out of the cabinet. He sorted through the four burgers, identified each, and placed them on their corresponding plates: The Double-Double was obviously his, with double the meat and more importantly, double the cheese (but no tomatoes or onions, please); the single burger with no cheese and no onions was for Lisa; and the double cheese with no meat and sauce only was for Keely. Kyle left Luke's burger in the box (single patty, cheese, no onion, no tomato, no pickles). It may have been Luke's usual order, but he was out tonight. Kyle was confident he'd be taking that one down, too.

He sprinkled each plate with a helping of French fries from the two orders of fries set into smaller trays in the larger box. He had just reached up to grab the salt from the cabinet when the hair on the back of his neck lifted.

He realized he was being watched.

Slowly, he removed the salt from the cabinet, set the shaker gently on the kitchen counter and then swirled suddenly, hooking his hands like talons and crying, "Booga, booga!"

Keely screamed a delightful little girl scream and yelled, "Daddy!" She made a tiny little fist and hit her father in the thigh. Kyle laughed.

"Scare you?"

"No!" Keely insisted.

"Yes, I did," Kyle said.

"No, you didn't."

"Then why'd you scream?"

"Cuz."

Kyle laughed. That was about the best answer he could get. "Here's your dinner, sweetheart," he said, passing Keely's plate to her. "You want milk?"

"No," Keely said. "Coke."

"How about juice?" Kyle asked. "I think we've got cranberry."

"Okay, daddy."

Kyle watched his daughter totter over to the La-Z-Boy chair, barely keeping her plate balanced. He thought about telling her *Hey, my chair!* but instead just smiled with fatherly love as he opened the refrigerator and poured her juice into a plastic Barbie cup.

A minute later, Lisa walked back in. "They get everything right?" she asked.

"Seems like it," Kyle said, handing her Keely's cup and nodding in her direction. Lisa walked over and handed it to Keely.

"Seems like we got an extra burger, too," Kyle said. "Considering that Luke's not going to be home."

"I got a feeling there won't be an extra burger for long," Lisa said.

They sat together and enjoyed their *In N Out* and watched *Toy Story 3* again for what seemed like the ninth time. But Kyle didn't care. MadeWest beer, awesome hamburgers, a movie that was truly one of the best ever made, and most of his family gathered together in the same room together. Life was good.

Oh, yeah, Kyle thought. *And no screeching phone calls, no writing on the wall and nobody telling us to leave our house now.*

Yeah. Life was good.

* * * * *

Later, after Woody, Buzz Lightyear and the rest had survived the trash compactor once again (a scene that Kyle wasn't sure Keely had seen even once since she'd always managed to fall asleep before the end of the film), Kyle carried his daughter to bed, tucked her in, and he and Lisa called it a night. They laid in bed, both on their backs staring up at the ceiling, and were having their traditional pre-slumber chat. Kyle knew he had scant minutes; Lisa had been known to fall asleep the moment her head hit the pillow.

"I'm still a little confused," Lisa said. "*Eraser dust? Rubber* eraser dust? How's that even possible."

Kyle shook his head. "I don't know," he said. "*They* didn't know. Their best guess is that somehow, it got buried beneath the skin and my body rejected it, causing an infection."

"And how much did he scrape out?"

"About a teaspoon full."

Lisa snorted. "How in the hell did you get a teaspoon full of rubber eraser shavings buried beneath your skin and not know it?"

"I know," Kyle agreed. "It's ridiculous." He had spent almost every minute of every hour since his appointment at Dr. Mayner's mulling over this. He knew of exactly two rubber erasers: one in his desk at work and one in the kitchen drawer at home. And he rarely used them. Even if he had, he had never used them anywhere near his ankle, for crissakes. It made absolutely no sense whatsoever.

"There is a bright side," Kyle said.

"I can't imagine."

"I might be featured in the New England Journal of Medicine," Kyle told her. "*The Amazing Rubber Heeled Pest Control Man.*"

That gave Lisa a laugh. "We'll be rich," she said.

"I'll probably get a TV endorsement deal from Ticonderoga. *Hi, I'm Kyle Callahan, the Amazing Rubber Heeled Pest Control Man. Let me tell you about the world's best #2 pencil.*"

They were both laughing now, giddily, the stress and confusion from the past week rolling off them in great gales of guffaws.

"Okay, okay," Lisa said after a few moments. "Stop, or we're gonna wake up Keely."

The laughter faded and, as expected, Kyle was not surprised to hear Lisa's breathing deepen and even out moments later. He smiled and shook his head. He'd never known anyone who could fall asleep so quickly. And he was envious.

He closed his eyes and just rested, trying not to think about everything that had happened over the past week. Of course, that was impossible. However, Kyle finally found the peace to drift off as he told himself *It's been calm and quiet since they took Mrs. Trellis away. Maybe everything's back to normal now.*

Chapter Twenty-Seven

The doorbell rang promptly at 2 o'clock and Lisa Callahan answered the door to find Eric Chambers on her doorstep along with a woman of about the same age at his side. Instantly, Lisa knew there was more to this couple than just a working relationship. Their style of rumpled scholarly clothing, their throwback appearance and their matching *bookishness* indicated they were somehow related. Probably husband and wife.

"Mrs. Callahan, it's good to see you," Chambers said, extending his hand. Lisa took it and shook it pleasantly.

"This is my wife, Becky. She's the psychic I told you about."

"Of course," Lisa said, shaking Becky's dry and bony hand and congratulating herself on her detective skills. "Glad to meet you, Becky," Lisa said. "And, please, both of you, call me Lisa. Come on in."

They entered. Lisa found it amusing that Chambers wore virtually the same ensemble he wore the night before: an out-of-date black suit (still dusty); black fedora (also dusty) but no scarf today. Becky was dressed correspondingly with black slacks that billowed around her thin legs like stage curtains, a lacy cream blouse and a dull gray sweater. Her longish brunette hair clung close to her skull and looked like it could use a wash.

"Can I get you something to drink?" Lisa asked. "A coffee? Soda? Water?"

"That won't be necessary," Chambers said.

"Water would be nice," Becky said. "I am a little thirsty."

"Perfect," Lisa told her. "I'll join you."

The front door entered into the living room, and it was just around the corner to the kitchen. Lisa led the scholarly couple to the refrigerator, opened it, and handed Becky a bottle of Dasani and took one for herself. "Would you like a glass?"

Becky shook her head. No.

Lisa raised her eyebrows at Chambers. "You're sure? Nothing?"

"No, thank you," Chambers said gracefully. "Is your husband home today?"

"No. He took Keely to the movies."

"That new Pixar film, I'll wager."

"You'd win," Lisa told him. "He loves those movies nearly as much as she does."

"As do I," Chambers said. "And your son?"

"At a friend's," Lisa told him. "Probably deep into another video game."

"What type of game does he prefer?" Chambers asked.

"He likes those sprawling alternate universe games," Lisa said. "You know, like *World of Warcraft,* some *Conan* game. Stuff like that."

"Ah. I was a huge *Dungeons and Dragons* player in my day," Chambers said.

I'll bet you were, Lisa thought.

Chambers reached into his coat pocket and came out with his notepad. "Shall we get started?" he asked, looking first at Lisa and then at Becky. Both women nodded. "Let's begin in the living room," Chambers said.

They walked back into the living room and Chambers made a point of going to each corner of the room where he paused and gazed up silently at the ceiling. Becky followed him, occasionally sipping from her water, sometimes cocking her head as if listening. Lisa wasn't sure if she should ask questions or offer information, so she decided just to keep quiet and see where things led.

"You've seen no activity in this room?" Chambers asked.

"Not that I'm aware of," Lisa told him.

"Becky, do you sense anything?"

Becky shook her head again. "No," she said simply. "Nothing at all."

"Very good," Chambers said. He turned to Lisa. "Now, please show us where the mysterious graffiti appeared."

They stepped over to the junction where the kitchen and living room met to form the hallway that led to the bedrooms. Lisa led them down to the master bedroom at the end of the hall and pointed to the area where *You must leave this house now* was written a few days before.

Chambers examined the area for a moment and then leaned close against the wall. He pressed his left ear flat against the paint and closed his eyes, listening carefully. He then stood back and rapped gently on the wall in several different areas, apparently judging the hollow tones made by his knuckles.

After a moment, he turned to Becky, whose eyes were fixated on the spot where the graffiti had appeared. "Becky?" he asked quietly.

Becky stared for a second longer and then closed her eyes, her forehead pinching in concentration. Abruptly, she opened them and told Chambers, "Nope. Nothing."

Chambers pursed his lips in surprise. "Interesting," he said. "Now, may I see the little girl's room?"

They walked back toward the kitchen toward Keely's room and entered. Lisa was a little embarrassed by the mess but figured, what the hell, she's only six, for crying out loud.

Chambers and Becky surveyed the room and Kyle once again did the corner searching routine. After a moment, he asked Lisa, "Can you show me where you saw the woman standing?"

"It was about right there," Lisa said. "Where you're standing. She was right there at the foot of the bed, staring down at Keely."

Chambers moved over so he was standing in the area Lisa was indicating. "And what was she doing?"

"Just standing there," Lisa told him. "Staring down at Keely."

"Was there any menace on her features?" Chambers asked. "Did she seem like she wanted to do the child harm?"

"Well, no," Lisa said. "In fact, it was almost the opposite. Like she was worried about her, maybe. Concerned."

"Very interesting," Chambers said. He moved out of the way and beckoned Becky to take his place. She moved forward and stood there quietly, staring down at where Keely would have been sleeping. After a few seconds, she closed her eyes, and her forehead wrinkled as she concentrated. She held that position for some time, long enough for Lisa to glance over at Chambers to see if there should be some concern. But then Becky once again abruptly opened her eyes and shook her head."

"Nope. Nothing."

They went through the same routine in every room, even the rooms where nothing bizarre had happened. Still, they found nothing. In each and every room, Becky got no response, felt no disturbance, no presence. Lisa was starting to get embarrassed. *Dammit, Gina*, she thought, *I told you we were overdoing this.*

But Chambers showed no signs of disappointment. He went from room to room eagerly and did not deflate each time Becky reported negatively.

Finally, they returned to the kitchen, where they sat at the dining room table and Chambers went over his notes. Lisa got Becky another water from the fridge and again offered Chambers a beverage, even telling him, "We've got some merlot," but Chambers politely declined.

The little spiral notepad had become quite a bit fuller, Lisa noticed, its pages swelling with the ink of many additional notes. Chambers appeared to have been doing his homework. Finally, he stopped at a particular page and tapped it with his finger.

"Mrs. Callahan," he said. "Didn't you say there was no basement here?"

"That's right," Lisa said. "There isn't."

"I was reviewing some historic records," Chambers said. "Going back some fifty years. Your house is over fifty years old, you know."

"Yes, we know that," Lisa said.

"Well, I was reviewing construction records and all of the homes that were built in this area at that time did indeed have basements."

"I can assure you we don't," Lisa said. "As I said, we've lived her for almost six years. We'd know if there was a basement. And the previous owner certainly never mentioned anything."

Chambers chewed on that a moment. "Are there any walk-in closets?" he asked. "You know, full size? A small room you can literally walk into, without any built-in shelves, etcetera?"

Lisa thought. "There are the closets in the bedrooms," she said. "The ones with the sliding doors."

"No. I'm talking about closets with normal doors. Doors with knobs."

Lisa nodded. "I guess there are two," she said. "There's the closet in the bedroom, where Kyle and I keep all of our clothes, and the broom closet in the back." She pointed through the kitchen to the small room where the washer and dryer were.

"Can you show me that broom closet, please?" Chambers asked.

"Sure." Lisa stood and walked through the kitchen into the laundry room. Lisa opened the door and stood back.

Chambers pressed past her and peered inside. It was a tiny room, a closet really, with the washer and dryer on the left with a small storage space on the right.

"Do you mind if I remove these items?" Chambers asked her, pointing at the vacuum cleaner, the sweeper, the broom and a few other cleaning items.

"Not at all," Lisa said.

Chambers began moving items out of the closet and passing them back to Lisa, who placed them on top of the washer. Soon, the closet was empty. Chambers stepped deeper inside and rapped his knuckles against the back wall, again listening closely. He moved to another section of the wall and rapped again. This time, his eyes squinted in puzzlement. He stepped back.

"Mrs. Callahan," he asked soberly. "May I?"

May you what? Lisa thought but quickly nodded yes.

Chambers stood back, lifted his foot off the floor (dusty black boots, Lisa noted) and then kicked at the back wall with all of his might. His foot broke through the wall easily and he pulled it back and kicked again.

"What are you doing?!" Lisa shrieked.

Chambers ignored her, kicking repeatedly, opening a huge hole in the wall. After a moment, Lisa saw something behind the broken wall.

It was a doorknob.

There was another door hidden behind the back wall of the broom closet.

Chambers stood back, breathing a little heavily, and pointed at the doorknob. "That is the door to your basement, madam, unless I am very much mistaken."

"I can't ..." Lisa mumbled. "I didn't ..."

Chambers nodded, reached forward and turned the knob. It turned easily under his grip, and it opened just as easily. A gust of cold, stale air blew in over them, issuing a kind of moan as it was released. Lisa felt goosebumps rise on her skin.

And then Becky screamed. It was a scream of pure horror, the scream of someone who has just witnessed a bloody murder or looked into the face of Satan himself. And then she dropped like a rag doll, passed out cold.

"Beck!" Chambers called. He closed the newly discovered basement door and rushed to Becky's side. She was already coming to, her eyes fluttering as she climbed back to consciousness.

Lisa knelt beside them, her heart pounding in her chest, her voice barely able to form words. "Is she all right?" she asked. "What happened?"

Chambers didn't respond. He held Becky close, staring down into her face, watching her lips move as she tried to form words. Finally, Becky croaked, "I'm all right. I just need some air."

Chambers and Lisa helped her to her feet, and they stepped out of the back door onto the patio. They stood over by the chain link fence that separated the Callahan home from the Trellis place, and Becky fell against it, looking exhausted and, Lisa thought, a little anemic.

"Are you all right?"

"Yes, I'm fine," Becky said, attempting a comforting smile but failing miserably. "Just a little overwhelmed."

"Did you sense something?" Chambers asked.

"Something hit me like a Mac truck," Becky said. "But I can't tell you what or why. It just hit me one moment and was gone the next."

Lisa asked again. "Can I get you anything?"

Becky managed a trembling smile. "Do you have any tea?" she asked. "I'd love a hot tea."

"Of course," Lisa said. She rushed back into the house and started opening cabinets, searching for tea bags. As she worked, she heard the Chambers talking outside. She couldn't make out their words, but she was certain they were talking about what had just happened. When she returned a few minutes later, with the hot tea in tow, she was surprised and pleased to see Becky standing on her own two feet, looking steady and gathered. Lisa pressed the tea into Becky's hand and Becky took it gratefully.

"Well, we just learned something rather significant," Chambers told Lisa.

"Really?" Lisa was pleased and curious. She glanced over at Becky, saw she was drinking her tea and seemed to be recovering nicely. Lisa felt a little better.

"Yes," said Chambers happily. "We've just learned that there used to be a school on these grounds, many years ago. I didn't come across anything about that in my research, so there's a new lead to follow."

"That's good," Lisa said, thinking, *I guess.* "How did you find this out?"

"We were just speaking with your neighbor, Miss Sutton," Chambers said.

Lisa felt a wave of confusion. "Miss Sutton?" she asked.

"Yes," Chambers confirmed. "She came out to see if we were okay. When I explained who we were and what we were doing here, she gave us a little history lesson."

"I'm sorry," Lisa said. "I don't know a Miss Sutton."

"She said she was your neighbor," Chambers told her.

"Yes, we just spoke to her," Becky added.

"Did she say where she lived?" Lisa asked. Maybe she was a neighbor from across the street. The Callahans lived on a corner and their only next-door neighbor was now in the hospital for what looked to be a dementia-related nervous breakdown.

"No, she didn't," Chambers said. "I just assumed you knew her."

Lisa ran through her list of neighbors. Mrs. Trellis lived next door, the Gerlachs were across the street and the

Rogers family lived next door to them. She could remember no family with the last name of Sutton.

Lisa shook her head. "Can you describe her for me? Miss Sutton?"

"I'm certain she said Sutton," Chambers replied, doubt starting to creep into his mind. "She's about your height, dark hair, pulled back in a bun today. And she was wearing a black dress with a white collar. Very conservative, like something an old school teach..." His voice trailed off.

"Like something an old schoolteacher might wear?" Lisa barely squeaked. A vision of the woman in Keely's room flashed through her mind, chilling her.

"Yes," Chambers said dully. "Something like that."

Lisa felt the world seem to blur around her. "That was the woman in Keely's room," she whispered.

Now it was Chambers turn to fall back against the chain link fence, his already pale features draining of what little blood was already there. "Good God, Becky," he said gravely. "I do believe we've seen our first genuine ghost."

CHAPTER TWENTY-EIGHT

"Really? We have a basement?" Kyle Callahan stood thunderstruck, staring at the ruined back wall of the broom closet and the brass doorknob hiding beneath. Lisa stood beside him, shaking her head at his boyish enthusiasm. He just couldn't wait to get down there and explore.

"That's what you come away with?" Lisa asked incredulously. "I tell you this amazing story about a ghost hunter and his psychic wife talking to a teacher's ghost in our own backyard, and all you can say is, 'We have a basement?'"

"You have to admit it's pretty cool," Kyle said. He stepped inside the closet and pried away more of the drywall. The opening was now almost big enough for a person to fit through.

"I don't know if 'cool' is the word I'd use," Lisa said. Kyle glanced back at her knowingly. Lisa realized that, despite the difficult afternoon and the panicked voicemail she'd left for him while he was still at the movies with Keely, Kyle probably sensed that she, too, was anxious to see their newly discovered basement.

"So, when is Mr. Ghost Hunter coming back again?" Kyle asked.

"He said he wanted to do some more research based on what the gh ... what Miss Sutton told him," Lisa said. "He said he'd call in a day or two."

"And when did you say the kids will be home?" Kyle asked.

"Keely's staying overnight at Nana's," Lisa said, using her kids' nickname for their grandmother. "And Kyle's over at The Armory, playing *World of Warcraft*. He probably won't be home until eleven."

"Perfect," Kyle said, grinning boyishly. "Wanna see what's down there?"

"No," Lisa said quickly but, when Kyle shot her a surprised glance, she nodded a reluctant yes.

Kyle pried away the remaining edges of the drywall blocking the hidden door, dropping the pieces on the already littered floor (*and who gets to clean that up?* Lisa thought) and reached for the knob. Once again, the door opened easily, and another hiss of stale frigid air wafted out from the other side.

As the air blew past her, Lisa heard Becky's scream in her head again, raising the fine hairs on the back of her neck. Suddenly, she didn't want to go down into that basement. But it was too late for that. Kyle had already stepped through the doorway. Not wanting to be left alone, Lisa quickly stepped closely behind him.

"Easy," Kyle said. "There's stairs here." He removed his flashlight from his belt (*The pest control expert's most important tool*, Lisa remembered him saying), clicked it on and flashed the beam down the stairway.

Lisa peered around him. Sure enough, a full-sized set of wooden stairs led down to what looked like a plain, gray cement floor. From their vantage point at the top of the stairs, the basement seemed completely empty, the only contents being spider webs, hanging heavy with dust, stretched across every square inch like a mad grand-mother's knitted blanket. It reminded Lisa of the set for a classic horror movie.

"Ready?" Kyle asked her.

No, Lisa thought. "Yes," she said aloud.

And they began down the stairway, Kyle stopping of-ten, testing each step before moving on. Lisa heard creaks and groans as Kyle's weight came down, but there was no threatening snap of cracking timber or the rattle of loose boards. They continued downward, Lisa staying as close to her husband, brushing away spiderwebs in disgust. Soon, they were on the basement floor.

Kyle flashed the light around the cellar. Lisa tried to follow the cone of light as it illuminated the room. Save for a single bulb hanging in the center of the cellar, the entire room was bare.

"Let's try that light," Kyle said, indicating the bulb. He stepped toward the center of the room and suddenly tripped, cursing.

"What is it?" Lisa cried.

"A hole or something," Kyle said. Lisa had visions of open graves littering the cellar floor and another chill ran through her.

Kyle got his footing and stepped more cautiously toward the dangling light bulb. He grabbed the chain there and gave it a yank. There was a pop, a hiss, and then the light flashed on, illuminating the cellar in a light brighter than Lisa would have imagined possible.

The first thing Lisa noticed was that, in fact, the room was virtually bare. It was your typical cellar: The walls were all plain gray cement, smooth and dull. The ceiling was a chessboard of crossing beams which Lisa understood were the support beams for the floor in the house above.

The cellar floor was also that same dull gray cement but the hole that Kyle had stepped in wasn't the only one. There were perhaps half a dozen depressions scattered throughout the room, sunken pits that varied in size from that of a shoe box to that of a small refrigerator. Lisa was reminded of an old graveyard she had visited in Ojai once. It had been built in the mid-1800s, and the graves there were so old that the coffins beneath had rotted and burst, collapsing the dirt above and creating a pit that looked like a giant axe had chopped the earth. Lisa remembered the electric creep of fear she had felt that day, looking down into that pit and realizing that a dead body, mummified or skeletal, was just below the surface. She felt that same creep of fear now.

"What are those holes in the floor?" she asked Kyle, proud of her ability to keep the trembling from her voice.

Kyle flashed his light on them. "Probably the graves of the victims of the serial killer who owned the house before us," he said.

"Ha ha," Lisa said. "Very funny."

Kyle laughed. Apparently, he thought it was funny. "Probably just washout," he said. "Soil beneath probably washed away and the cement collapsed. Not too many of them, probably nothing to worry about."

Kyle clicked off the flashlight and hung it back on his belt. "Well, that was a little disappointing," he said. "I was hoping we'd find Capone's vault down here or something."

Lisa laughed. "Yeah, right," she said. "Capone's vault in sunny Southern California."

"Hey, he did end up in Alcatraz," Kyle said.

"That's a long way from Ventura County," Lisa told him.

Kyle took out his flashlight again and flashed it around the darker corners. "You know," he said. "A little paint, a sofa, a TV and a lava lamp and this would make a great office for me."

"If by office, you mean man cave," Lisa said.

Kyle laughed again. "Seriously, we can use this space," he said. "Get this place cleaned up and store food down here, or something."

"Or something," Lisa said, hugging her shoulders. "Let's go back upstairs. It's cold down here."

Kyle nodded, returned his flashlight to his belt, and pulled the beaded chain, killing the single bulb, and leaving them in darkness. Together, they climbed the stairs toward the light.

Chapter Twenty-Nine

Luke called at about ten o'clock and asked if he could stay the night at Bradshaw's again. Lisa gave him permission but told him it would be the last time this week; she didn't want Bradshaw's mom to think they were taking advantage of her. Luke assured her that wasn't the case and hang up abruptly. Lisa smiled.

"So," she told Kyle, who was sitting in the kitchen browsing sports scores on his iPad. "The kids aren't coming home tonight. What do you say we watch an R-rated movie, split some nachos, drink some maggies and get a little frisky?"

Kyle touched the off switch on the iPad. "I think that sounds like my kind of evening," he said.

It was *nice*, Lisa thought later, basking in the afterglow, feeling her eyelids grow heavy already. They had first adjourned to the living room where they had sat on the sofa together and watched the latest Paul Rudd comedy on HBO, Kyle absently rubbing Lisa's bare feet. While they watched, and between foot rubs, Lisa had made a plate of nachos with chili beans and lots of cheese and a pair of her signature margaritas to go along with it. The cocktails did the trick, and it wasn't long after the movie was over that they had found themselves in bed, wrapped naked in each other's arms.

It was nice, Lisa thought again, and promptly drifted off to sleep.

* * * * *

The digital clock beside the bed silently announced in broken red numbers that it was 2:31 in the morning. Lisa found herself awake. She lay there a moment, staring up at the ceiling (which she could barely see in the darkness) and wondered what had woken her. It was usually Kyle's snoring. The man made more noise asleep than most Rottweilers did while fighting other Rottweilers. Lisa swore that sometimes he made the windows rattle. But Kyle was almost silent, sound asleep beside her, his back to her. She reached out and let her hand ride the swelling of his ribcage as he breathed and slept peacefully.

She thought again of Rottweilers and mused that maybe it was a barking dog that had awakened her. Sometimes the Gerlach's dog, Scruffy, got started—barking at a possum or just somebody walking down the street—and it seemed like he would never shut the hell up. Lisa listened carefully, but didn't hear a dog, or anything else really, except for the normal creaking of the house settling. *Seems to have been a lot of that lately,* Lisa thought.

Dickens' "A Christmas Carol" came to her mind. Maybe it was an undigested bit of beef, a blot of mustard, a crumb of cheese or a fragment of underdone potato that woke her up. Or, in this case, an undigested bit of ground beef, a blot of Tapatio, a crumb of nacho cheese or a fragment of tortilla chip. *Damn those nachos are good,* Lisa thought, *but they can play havoc with my digestive system.*

She considered getting up and chewing some Tums, but it was warm under the blankets, and she didn't feel the usual mild burn in her stomach that had woken her up in the past, so she decided just to soldier through and try to get back to sleep. She rolled over onto her side, rested her hand on Kyle's side again, took a deep breath …

…and felt it catch in her throat.

Because she was suddenly aware that somebody was watching her from the open bedroom door. She could see the pale oval moon of their face in the darkness of the doorway.

"Luke?" she said weakly, hopefully and doubtfully.

Suddenly, it was no longer warm under the blankets as that pale oval crept closer, and Lisa could see that it was *indeed* a face, the face of the woman she had seen days before in Keely's room. The same pale skin, the same jet-black hair pulled back in a scholarly bun and the same lace-collared black dress that Lisa now realized looked like something out of a vintage photo.

Miss Janet Sutton.

The woman glided slowly but purposefully into the room and, although Lisa couldn't see the woman's eyes in the shadows, she knew that they were looking directly at her. She tried to give Kyle a little shake, tried to wake him, but her arm wouldn't move.

At last, the woman approached the edge of the bed and, in the light of the red digital letters from the alarm clock, Lisa could see her face clearly now. The woman's alabaster skin was nearly perfect, her eyes a deep brown. Her hair was straight and well-maintained and the look on her face was the same Lisa had seen in Keely's room … a look of troubled concern.

"You must leave this house now," the woman whispered, and she raised her hand and pointed directly at Lisa's face.

"Kyle!" The name exploded out of Lisa's mouth like a bat out of a cave at sunset. "Kyle! Wake up! She's here! She's here!"

Lisa's arm came alive, and she grabbed Kyle's shoulder and shook it roughly as the woman lifted her other arm and reached for Lisa, her fingertips getting closer, her hands hooking into talons. "You must leave this house now," the woman said again, more urgently, her voice a low growl now. Her face began to tighten with frustration and anger.

"Kyle!" Lisa screamed, "Kyle!"

Finally, Kyle awoke. He calmly rolled over to face Lisa, as thought he had all the time in the world, as though the woman wasn't even in the room, and Lisa looked into his eyes and a cry of pure terror leapt from her throat. There were no words, just a pure stream of unadulterated horror screeching from her vocal cords with unstoppable force.

Because Kyle's face was no longer there. Instead, it was a mass of oily brown bed bugs shaped like a face, squirming and roiling and crawling over one another. The nose was there, the eyes were there, the mouth was there but they were built of active bed bugs. And the oily brown lips parted and a voice—not Kyle's but not unlike Kyle's—asked sweetly, "What is it, honey? What's wrong?"

The scream caught in Lisa's throat and she realized she couldn't breathe. Her eyes widened and tears spilled from them as she felt something in her chest give and then she succumbed to the darkness.

And then, as though somebody had flipped a switch, Lisa found herself back in bed, back staring at the nightstand where the digital clock told her it was 3:45am. Her body was painted in a sheen of sweat and her eyes stung from the saltiness that dripped into her eyes. She could feel her heart pounding away furiously in her chest and found it difficult to catch her breath.

She lay there a moment, calming herself.

Kyle slept quietly beside her, undisturbed. Lisa wanted to reach out and touch him but was terrified at what she might see if he awakened and turned toward her.

The black rectangle of the doorway was empty.

Jesus Christ, Lisa thought. *That was some freaking nightmare.*

She allowed her pulse and breathing to return to normal and then cautiously eased out of bed. She padded into the master bathroom and poured herself a glass of water, leaving the light off so as not to disturb Kyle. The frosty night air cooled the sweat on her skin.

Lisa stepped out of the bathroom and was almost back to bed when she saw her. Miss Sutton. The woman from Keely's room, the woman from her nightmare, now standing at the edge of the bed near Kyle. She looked up at Lisa with that same look of quiet concern and she whispered again, "You must leave this house…"

And Lisa lost it. "No!" she screamed. "No! This is *our* house! Get the hell out of here! Get out of *our* house!" She felt the anger ball up in her like a giant fist and she raced toward the woman, who appeared unaware of Lisa's current state of rage. "Get out!" Lisa screamed again, "Get the hell out!"

Lisa pulled back her arm, drew back her fist and was just about to deliver a blow when the woman abruptly vanished. Disappeared, like a hologram whose power has just been cut off. Lisa stumbled through the now empty space, the momentum of the punch pulling her through, and caught herself on the nightstand on Kyle's side of the bed.

"What?" Kyle said groggily, his eyes blinking rapidly as he propped himself up on his elbows. "What is it? What's going on?" He stared at his wife through sleep-heavy eyes. "You scared the hell out of me."

Lisa choked a little laugh at the irony of that, and then she broke down sobbing.

Chapter Thirty

It was 4:21 in the morning, and Lisa and Kyle Callahan were in the kitchen, drinking coffee, and trying to calm each other down.

"You're sure you're all right?" Kyle asked.

"I'm not all right," Lisa replied. "But I'm better."

"What the hell is going on here?" Kyle said. "I mean, this has been one weird freaking week."

"Tell me about it," Lisa said.

"Should we call that Chambers guy?"

"Honey, it's four in the morning. I'm not sure Mr. Chambers would appreciate a phone call at this hour."

"I don't care," Kyle said. "This has got to stop."

"We're not even sure he can stop it."

"I know that. But what other options do we have?"

They sat quietly, their minds working.

"What about a priest?" Lisa said. "Exorcising the house?"

"You know that's not going to work," Kyle said.

"*I* know that," Lisa said. "But maybe our ghost doesn't."

"I guess we're at that stage," Kyle said. "Throw everything at the wall, see what sticks. Worse comes to worse, we can always move."

"We're *not* moving," Lisa said. She banged her coffee cup on the table, sloshing some of its contents onto a paper napkin there. "Screw that bitch. She's not forcing me out of my home." She took another sip of coffee, then slammed the cup down again. "If she wasn't already dead, I'd fucking kill her."

They were quiet for a moment, and then Kyle started laughing silently. Lisa could tell he was trying not to, but he couldn't help himself.

"What the hell's so funny?" she asked, punching him on the arm.

"Nothing," he managed. "Nothing." He tried to hold back another laugh, but it came out a snort instead. "'If she wasn't already dead, I'd fucking kill her'," he repeated. And he could hold back the laughter no longer.

Lisa tried to be mad, but now she was laughing, too. She realized what it might look like if one of their neighbors could see them. The Callahans, sitting at their kitchen table at half past four in the morning, sipping coffee, talking of ghosts, both in pajamas, and laughing like idiots. It took a little sting out of the situation, and Lisa appreciated it.

BANG! Suddenly, there was a huge crack from beneath them and the house lurched sharply. Dishes rattled in the cupboards and Lisa was sure she could hear the silverware ringing in the drawers. A cupboard over the stove opened and the Callahans' supply of Tylenol and Advil spilled out onto the kitchen floor.

Lisa sat, wide-eyed, as the rumbling came to a stop. Her coffee had slopped all over her hand and she could feel the stinging burn. She looked over at Kyle who sat stock still in his chair, as wide-eyed as she was.

Neither of them was laughing now.

Lisa stood up. She arched her back, raised her hands in the air, and extended the middle fingers on each one. "Screw you, bitch!" she called out loudly. "You're not kicking me out of my own house!"

The house answered with complete silence.

Then Lisa noticed that Kyle's shoulders were shaking with stifled laughter again. She punched him in the arm, harder this time, and asked, "What? What's so goddamn funny?"

"If I was that ghost," Kyle said between snickers, "I'd get the hell out of here like yesterday!"

Chapter Thirty-One

Lisa waited until what she thought was a decent hour for a Sunday, 8:15 in the morning, and called Eric Chambers. She stood with her back to the sink, coffee in one hand, the phone in the other.

"Mrs. Callahan!" Chambers said enthusiastically upon hearing her voice. "I was going to call you today ..."

"Listen," Lisa said, cutting him off. "We've got to get the ball rolling on this. I had a very bad experience last night."

"Really?" Chambers said, his voice suddenly serious and fiercely interested. "Tell me about it."

And Lisa did, feeling her skin prickle over with goose-bumps at the worst parts and leaving out anything about her screaming profanities at the ghost. When she finished, Chambers' tone was sober.

"Mrs. Callahan, I am not telling you to move out of your house," he said. "But for the next couple of nights, may I suggest you and the family stay in a hotel somewhere."

"Why?"

"It seems that you have what I call an 'escalating haunting.' What that means, is that this haunting is leading up to an event, a cataclysmic event that could cause you and your family harm."

Lisa's heart skipped a beat. "I thought you said that ghosts couldn't hurt us," she said.

"I still believe that to be the case," Chambers told her. "By 'cataclysmic,' I don't necessarily mean physical. What I mean is that the events you have witnessed so far will increase in frequency and in intensity until you are *forced* to relinquish the property."

Bring it on, bitch, Lisa thought. *You're not forcing me to do anything.*

But then she thought of the children. They were the main concern, of course, and it was of the utmost importance that they were safe. She wouldn't move her family out of their house and home, but if they had to spend a few days in a hotel somewhere, so be it. "Okay," she told Chambers. "We'll consider it. What do we do in the meantime?"

"I'd like to come over today to share some of my research with you. Are you available?"

"Just name a time," Lisa said. "We'll be there."

"How does eleven sound?"

"That'll work."

"Splendid," Chambers said. "I'd very much like to meet your husband, too."

"He'll be there," Lisa said. "Speaking of which, how is Becky doing today?"

"She's fine," Chambers told her. "Right as rain. We look forward to seeing you later today."

"Us, too," Lisa said. "We've got to put this thing to bed."

"We are working on it, Mrs. Callahan," Chambers said. "Please rest assured, we are working on it."

They said their goodbyes and Lisa poured herself another cup of coffee, blowing on it to cool the surface before taking a sip. Suddenly, the front door burst open, hard enough to smack against the wall with a resounding thump! Lisa flinched and just managed not to spill any of the hot coffee.

"Mommy!" Keely called, running into the kitchen and throwing her arms around her.

"Good morning, Kit Kat," Lisa said, ruffling her daughter's hair. "How was Nana's?"

"Fun, fun, fun!" Keely said. "We had pizza, we watched TV, and we played Monster High!" Keely held up her Abbey Bominable doll and wiggled it in Lisa's face, then ran out of the kitchen toward her room, nearly crashing into Andrea, Lisa's mother, who had just stepped in.

"You look like hell," Andrea told Lisa.

"Thanks for that, mom," Lisa said. "It was a rough night."

"In a good way or bad way?" Andrea asked coyly.

Lisa smiled. "Little of both," she said.

"Everything okay?"

"Sure. Just a little hectic." She nodded toward the coffee pot. "Coffee?"

"No, thanks, honey, I've got to get going," Andrea said. "Yoga class at ten."

"Yoga on Sunday?" Lisa asked.

Andrea nodded. "Yep. One on one with Arturo. Costs me seventy-five bucks a pop, but he's gorgeous so it's worth it."

"I should've known," Lisa said, rolling her eyes. Her mother had become notorious for gallivanting with young men a few years after her husband, Lisa's father, had died. *What the hell*, Lisa figured. *Gives her something to do.* She snickered. *Gives her* someone *to do.*

"Thanks for taking Keely last night," Lisa told her, and gave her mom a hug. "It was a big help."

"No worries. I love that little pumpkin."

"I know." Lisa told her. "Have fun with Arturo."

Andrea winked. "I will." She headed out the front door.

Lisa sat at the kitchen table, rubbed her eyes with the heel of her hands and sat back. She was exhausted. She wanted nothing more than to hit the sheets and sleep straight through until ... well, until all this ghost bullshit was over.

She took another drink of coffee and glanced at the wide-eyed cat clock on the wall. Its tail swayed saucily, and its eyes danced to the left and to the right. It was almost 8:30am. Time to take a shower, get dressed for the day and get her act together. And where the hell was Kyle and her McDonald's? How did that man expect her to get on with her day without her Sunday Bacon Biscuit?

CHAPTER THIRTY-TWO

The Chambers arrived promptly at 11 o'clock and, once again, Lisa was not surprised to find Chambers wearing the same dusty clothing he had worn the day before, including his ever-present fedora. Becky, however, wore what looked like a freshly laundered white blouse and black jeans. She looked refreshed and lively, and Lisa was glad to see that.

Lisa introduced her husband who shook hands all around and then invited everyone to the living room where they took seats around the coffee table. The Callahans took the sofa and the Chambers sat in two chairs brought in from the dining room.

"Lisa told you about last night?" Kyle asked Chambers.

"Yes, indeed," Chambers replied. "A very frightening chain of events, I'm sure."

"Woke me up out of a sound sleep," Kyle told him. "There's not much more frightening than having your wife screaming her head off in the middle of the night."

"I can imagine," Chambers continued. "But I think I may have the very beginnings of a grasp on what's going on here."

"We're all ears," Lisa replied.

Chambers dug into a weathered leather satchel he'd brought and pulled out three manila folders. He opened the first one and removed a black-and-white photo. Lisa guessed it had been printed on Chambers' home printer, based on the way the heavy ink had warped the paper.

"As I told you before, my initial research didn't reveal much on your home and the surrounding areas prior to the year it was built, fifty-odd years ago. We found info on the public pool that had been there in the late 1800s, but there was nothing more. Except that there had been homes there. But then I dug a little deeper, spending hours …"

"… *eight* hours," Becky clarified.

"…at the library, poring through microfiche copies of old newspapers. And I discovered this."

He slid the photograph on the table over to the Callahans. Lisa picked it up and scanned it, with Kyle looking over her shoulder.

It was an old photo, very old, judging from the sepia tone and the style of clothing worn by those pictured. The photo showed six children: three young boys in the forefront, and three girls of the same age in the background, sitting at desks in a classroom. All the boys wore suspenders, and their hair was cropped close and neat. The girls were harder to see, hidden behind the boys but, from what Lisa could see, they wore simple dresses and had their hair pulled up and clipped away from their necks.

But what made Lisa's pulse quicken and her breath shorten was the teacher standing in front of them. She wore a startlingly familiar black dress, a lace collar encircled her throat, and her black hair was drawn back into a bun and tucked beneath a small, square cap made mostly of white netting. Her alabaster skin looked perfect even in the old photograph and, although they were only black dots in the photos, Lisa knew the eyes were a deep brown.

"That's her," she said, softly tapping the photo. "That's the woman I saw."

Kyle leaned closer, then absently touched the woman's image in the photo. "That's her? Are you sure?

"I'm sure," Lisa said, and she'd never been more sure of anything in her life.

"Her name is Janet Sutton," Chambers announced. "She was the teacher at the Jefferson Schoolhouse, which originally sat almost exactly where your home sits today."

"When was that?" Kyle asked. Lisa was thinking the same question but couldn't take her eyes off the woman in the photo.

"1899," Chambers said. "Near the turn of the century."

"Oh, my god," Lisa said. "I can't believe what I'm seeing. Where did you find this?"

"It was in one of the newspapers I discovered at the library," Chambers said.

"That's the same woman we spoke to yesterday," said Becky. "I've no doubt of it."

"Wait a second," Kyle said. "You *spoke* to her?"

"As I have told your wife, Mr. Callahan, ghosts are not necessarily the ethereal images you see in the movies. They more often look exactly like you or me. You have probably seen many ghosts in your lifetime but were unaware of what they were because you were taught to expect something else entirely."

Kyle nodded in understanding. "Actually, I had a friend," he said. "Who was the director of a small movie they shot out in Oxnard. They shot the movie at an old restaurant—I forget the name—that they were told was haunted."

Lisa remembered this story and knew where Kyle was going. She had never believed it herself but after the events of the past week, there was no doubt now that the story was true.

"Anyway, they only had the restaurant for two days, so they were shooting 24 hours a day. In the middle of the night, like at three in the morning, my friend was in the back working by himself. Suddenly, the back door of the restaurant opened, and this guy walked in. My friend was shocked because they had made sure all the doors were locked. So, anyway, this guy comes in … this tall, thin, drunk guy … and he told my friend he just wanted to buy a drink. Well, my friend politely told him that he had to leave because the restaurant had been closed for hours. But the guy insisted, insisted he just wanted to come in for a drink. Finally, my friend convinced him to leave." He gave them a look, and Lisa felt he was gauging their belief in the story he was telling. "Anyway, the rest of the team came back into that room after the shot was finished and my friend told them the story. They were shocked and thrilled because, apparently, *that was the ghost*! That was exactly what the ghost had done to other people who had been seen him in the past."

Chambers nodded. "That is precisely what I'm talking about, Mr. Callahan. Ghosts don't look like sheets with holes cut out for the eyes. They more often look like you and me. And they don't often make a habit of scaring people unless there's something they want."

"And the fact that Janet Sutton was a teacher also tells us something," Becky volunteered. "Ghosts often use the same tools in the afterlife that they used when they were alive. Miss Sutton was a teacher. Consider your events here: the chalk warning in the hallway. Chalk, like a teacher would use on a blackboard. The phone calls. Didn't you say it sounded like nails on a chalkboard?"

Kyle nodded.

"The eraser infection in your heel," Becky continued. "Like the eraser rubbings left over by those pink pencil erasers." She shook her head in disbelief. "We've never seen anything like *that*, I can promise you."

"Yes," Chambers confirmed. "That was a new one."

"And there's this," Chambers said, a little too delightfully for Lisa's taste. "I also did a little research on your neighbor, Mrs. Trellis."

"And?"

"And guess what she did for a living when she was still among the workforce?"

"You've got to be kidding," Kyle said.

"I am not," Chambers declared. "She was a teacher. I cannot say for certain, obviously, that that had anything to do with her breakdown, but I find the coincidence quite compelling."

"I would say so," Kyle agreed.

"That doesn't explain the bed bugs," Lisa added. "Or the gophers."

"Hauntings often involve those things important to the victims," Chambers said. "Obviously, you being a pest control expert, Mr. Callahan, led to the incidents with the bed bugs and the gophers. Usually, however, they are inspired by traumatic events. Have you had any traumatic experiences with either bed bugs or gophers?"

Kyle and Lisa nodded together, their eyes wide. "There was an apartment complex we were servicing for bed bugs a few years back," Kyle said. "Worst infestation I'd ever seen. We were going door to door, treating each room for the bugs—*cinches*, the tenants called them. We're required by law to post intent to treat at least 24 hours prior to doing so even though we usually ask for more time because of the preparation required. But as we were treating this hallway and I came to a door that still had our notice taped to it."

Lisa squirmed. She had heard this story many times before and knew where it was going. It had been years ago, but the horror still stuck in her mind.

"We knocked on the door, we pounded on the door, hoping the tenant would answer. But he never did. We noticed bed bugs literally crawling into the hallway from beneath the door. When you see something like that," Kyle said. "You know you've got a bad infestation."

"Go on," Chambers prompted.

"Well, we finally got the super to open the door and I went in first. The place smelled like death, and I have never in my entire career seen so many bed bugs in one room. They were all over the walls, they covered the floor, they were on everything. I called out, 'Jalama Pest Control,' several times but got no answer. It seemed that nobody was home."

Kyle took a breath. Steadied himself. Lisa could see the horror of what he was about to tell them welling up in his eyes again, after all these years.

"Anyway, I went into the bedroom and that's where I found him. The tenant. He had been dead for a few days, they determined later—from a stroke apparently—and he was laying half in and half out of the bed. He looked like one of those zombies from *The Walking Dead*. And the bed bugs had *feasted* on him. They covered every inch of his skin, and they were fat and bloated and it was the most disgusting and horrifying thing I have ever seen."

Kyle stopped short, taking another breath to steady himself. Lisa patted his hand.

"That is indeed a horrible story," Chambers agreed solemnly. "But it explains why Miss Sutton opted to taunt you with the bed bugs." He pursed his lips for a moment, and then asked. "I am sorry to ask you this: But what about gophers? Have you had any traumatic incidents with gophers?"

"Not really," Kyle said. "I just hate the little bastards. I hate them a lot."

Chambers laughed. "That may be your answer right there," he said. "Miss Sutton picked up on your hatred of the rodents and used them to get your attention."

"Get our attention?" Lisa asked nervously. "What does this Janet Sutton want from us?"

"Obviously, she wants you to leave the house," Chambers said. "It is *why* she wants you to leave that we don't know, and that's probably the most important thing. But now that we know her name and know her face, I have something more to go on. I will continue my research the moment we finish here, and I will find something, I promise you." He paused, pursing his lips again. "What I find most interesting here is that there is no mention of this school in local history books, in the museum in which I work, or pretty much anywhere else for that matter. If I hadn't gone through all those newspapers page by page, I would have never known it existed. And I pride myself on my knowledge of this city and its history."

"Why would that be?" Lisa asked. "There must be something."

"I'm sure there is," Chambers said. "I just have to find it. The last record I found of Miss Sutton's school was an ice cream social held in 1901, two years after that photo was taken."

Lisa looked down at the photo again, at the image of the long-dead Janet Sutton staring back at her with those grainy black eyes.

"So, what's the plan?" Kyle asked.

"The plan, sir, is that I must hit the library again."

"It's Sunday," Kyle said. "The library is closed."

Chambers smiled knowingly. "There are some benefits to being the director of the local history museum," he said. "I have friends in high places. The library is not closed to me."

"So, what do we do?" Kyle asked.

"Have you given any thought to moving to a hotel?" Chambers said. Lisa shrugged.

"A little," she said. "I think it's a good idea, but I haven't discussed it with Kyle yet."

"I would advise it," Chambers said. "I don't believe you're in any physical danger here, but the mental anguish is unnecessary."

Lisa nodded slowly.

"Thank you again for your time and effort on this," Kyle said, standing and shaking Chambers' hand. Chambers and Becky rose as well.

"There is one thing," Chambers said. "Before we leave, Becky would like to see the basement."

Lisa and Kyle exchanged glances. "Do you think that's wise?" Lisa asked.

"I asked her the same question," Chambers said.

"And I told him I was fine," Becky insisted. "Whatever happened here yesterday was a one-time fluke. And I think it's important that I get a feel for what's down there."

"If you're okay with it," Kyle said.

"I am," Becky confirmed.

They walked in tandem to the laundry room and Kyle opened the broom closet door. He reached through, grasped the knob on the other side and turned it. Once again, the door swung open easily and once again a breath of cold, musty air blew past them. This time, however, Becky didn't blink.

"Shall we?" Chambers said, offering his palm. Becky took his hand.

"Yes," Becky said bravely. But Lisa could see a little fear in her eyes.

Once again, they used Kyle's professional grade flashlight to maneuver their way to the single bulb, Kyle telling them to be wary of the holes in the basement floor. He pulled on the chain and the plain gray room was exposed in all its dullness. If anything, it seemed even more boring and efficient than before.

Chambers repeated his corners routine, removing his camera and taking several snaps of each wall and the point where it connected with the ceiling and the floor. He stepped gingerly over the gaping holes in the floor, snapping pictures of those as well.

Becky moved to the far corner of the room, to the darkest area of the cellar. Lisa silently prayed that they wouldn't trip in one of the pits and sue them. *Ghosts I can deal with*, she thought, *Ghosts and lawyers maybe not.*

After a moment, Chambers put his camera away and focused on Becky. She stood with her head back and her eyes closed, a look of total concentration coming over her.

A few seconds passed, and then her eyes popped back open.

"Anything?"

She nodded gently. "Something," she said. "Not much." She closed her eyes again, concentrating deeply. "It's strange," she said after a moment, "I get a sense of anxiety, or concern. It's not intense, but it's ... it's there."

Chambers shrugged. "Well, it was good to see it," he said. "You know, this might make a nice family room."

"Yeah, that's what I said," Kyle agreed. "Once I fix up the holes. Thanks for finding it, by the way."

Chambers smiled and nodded. "You are welcome."

They returned upstairs, Kyle closing both the cellar door and the broom closet door behind him. They said their goodbyes and made promises to report to one another if anything should come up.

Kyle and Lisa watched the Chambers drive away in their little Ford sedan. *I hope they know what they're doing*, Lisa thought. Or we're screwed.

As she and Kyle went back into the house, Lisa found herself thinking about the basement. Had there been an additional hole in the ground there that wasn't there yesterday? Or was it just her imagination? She put the thought out of her mind. She hadn't bothered to count and certainly, another hole couldn't have just appeared there overnight.

CHAPTER THIRTY-THREE

"So, what do you think?" Lisa was standing by the sink, washing a bag of lettuce, preparing for dinner. Kyle stood behind her at the stove, warming a pot of Campbell's Hearty Cheeseburger Soup, his favorite.

"Think about what?" Kyle asked.

"Finishing dinner, packing up the kids, and high-tailing it to a hotel tonight?"

For once, both Luke and Keely were home. Keely sat in the living room watching *My Little Pony* on Netflix, while Luke was kicking back on his bed, absently strumming the Ovation guitar his parents had given him for Christmas last year. *All those lessons*, Kyle thought, *and all he can play* is "Smoke on the Water."

"I think it's probably too late tonight," Kyle said. "The kids both have school tomorrow and, by the time we eat, it'll be almost eight o'clock. And we still have to get them bathed and in bed. And we'd still have to pack and then find a hotel that's got a vacancy."

"It's Sunday night," Lisa said. "There'll be a vacancy."

"I don't want to stay at Bristol Hotel with the kids, do you?" Kyle said. It seemed that particular hotel was in the papers every morning, either for someone getting robbed, beaten or, occasionally, even shot.

"Not the hotel I was thinking of," Lisa said. "The Crown Plaza is nice, and it's not that expensive."

Kyle rolled the dice. "Let's stick it out tonight," he said. "Get everyone ready. We'll get packed and take whatever else we need and then move to the Crown Plaza tomorrow."

"How long do you think we'll be there?" Lisa said sadly.

"Not too long," Kyle said. "I hope."

They finished making dinner and called the kids to the table. As expected, they both complained about the soup and salad meal, Keely insisting she wanted hot dogs and Luke saying he was sick of rabbit food. They both ate what was on their plates, however, thanks to the magic of ketchup and croutons. The family cleaned up the after-dinner mess together, the adults washing the dishes, the children drying them and putting them away. *They used to bitch about that, too*, Lisa said. *I guess now they're used to it. Maybe one day they'll get used to 'rabbit food.'*

When the dishes were all clean and put away in their proper places, the family dispersed, Luke heading off to his room, Keely to the living room in front of the TV as usual, and mom and dad to the bedroom where they packed enough clothes to last them three days.

Lisa was looking forward to the stay. The Crown Plaza was a very nice hotel. It was right on the beach near the world-famous Ventura Pier, and the promenade made for great walking except after dark when the criminal element too often made their appearance. There were great restaurants not only inside the hotel but nearby, including one of

Lisa's favorites, the Aloha Steakhouse. And one of Kyle's favorites, Barrelhouse 101, was right across the street. *If we have to stay at a hotel for a few days*, Lisa thought, *I'm glad we're staying there.*

When they were finished packing their bags, Lisa went into Keely's room and packed her daughter's luggage. They went together into Luke's room, knowing the teenager demon would make at least a brief appearance and they were not disappointed. "*I'm not wearing that*," Luke snarled at them, when Lisa started to pack a plain orange t-shirt for him. "That shirt is stupid." Thankfully, Luke was more deeply involved in his videogame than the packing being done, and Lisa simply threw the orange shirt aside, wondering how a shirt could be stupid, and finished packing with no further incident.

The last thing Lisa packed was her make-up, having to make the difficult decision of what she would need in the morning versus what she could pack now. Of course, packing the make-up bag took the most time and it didn't help that Kyle playfully needled her about it throughout the entire process. Finally, though, everyone was packed and ready for tomorrow.

Keely chose that moment to totter into the bedroom, rubbing her eyes and holding Abbey Bomnible by one clawed plastic hand. "Daddy, will you read to me now?" she asked. "I'm tired." Lisa could see the exhaustion in her daughter's eyes.

"You bet, honey!" Kyle said, scooping up his daughter. "Let's go see what Charlie and Willy are up to tonight! Give mommy a kiss." He dipped his daughter close so that Lisa could give her a quick kiss goodnight and then they were out of the room, off to tales of the Chocolate Factory.

Lisa sat on the bed a moment, thinking she'd forgotten something. *Toothbrushes! Dammit!* She went into the bathroom, opened the cabinet under the sink and grabbed their two travel toothbrushes, snug in their orange plastic containers, from the cup there. She went back into the bedroom, unzipped her make-up bag and stuffed the two brushes inside. It was difficult to zip back up, but Lisa was confident they now had everything they needed.

A moment later, Kyle poked his head in the door. "She's already out," he said. "Join me for a cocktail?"

"I thought you'd never ask," Lisa said, and followed Kyle to the kitchen. He poured a glass of chardonnay for her and popped open an IPA for himself. Lisa made a face. "How can you drink that stuff at this time of the night?"

"I can drink this stuff *any* time," Kyle laughed. "Hey, is there anything to snack on?" He opened the fridge and bent down to explore its contents.

"What? You didn't get enough rabbit food?" Lisa joked. "I think there's some string cheese in there."

Kyle closed the refrigerator door and displayed the gorgeous red apple he'd noticed there earlier in the week. "Split an apple with me?" he said.

"Sure," Lisa replied.

Kyle took the apple over the counter and withdrew a butcher knife far too big for splitting a single apple. "Hey, when did you buy this?" he asked, displaying the apple. "I swear this thing looks better than the first time I saw it in there."

"I didn't get it," Lisa said. "I thought you brought it."

"Not me," Kyle said, and he drew the knife through the apple, cutting it into two nearly perfect halves. As good as the apple looked, however, Kyle noticed that the white meat of the apple was threaded with a brown ribbon. *Worm?* He picked one half of the apple up and looked closer.

It was no worm. It was some sort of rot. Kyle's breath caught in his throat, and he held the apple, flat side out, to show his wife. "Lisa …" he choked.

Lisa looked up at Kyle, alarmed. It looked as though he had just seen a … well, a ghost. She saw the rot in the apple and her first thought was *eeewww*, but that thought was obliterated a split second later.

Because the rot wasn't some randomly growing decomposition. Instead, it curled and rolled and intentionally spelled out a phrase in English.

Inside the white meat of the apple, the brown rot spelled the sentence: "You must leave this house now."

And then all hell broke loose.

CHAPTER THIRTY-FOUR

Eric Chambers slid the key into the vintage padlock hanging on the gate at the Ventura Historical Museum and it popped open with a metallic clank. It had been Chambers' idea to secure the outside gate with the ornate lock discovered in an old home on the Avenue downtown. He thought it would be fitting. That, and the cast iron lock was heavy and solid and there wasn't a crowbar made that could pry it from its perch.

Chambers moved next to the front door of the adobe-type building and opened it with another key on his porcupine keyring. As he entered the building, the alarm system began beeping a warning. Chambers knew he had about thirty seconds to enter his code and turn off the alarm before the sirens started wailing and he efficiently did so in about fifteen. There was little he hated more than the scream of those sirens in the middle of the night or first thing in the morning. They were shrill and obnoxious as, he supposed, they should be.

Chambers could feel exhaustion creeping into every nook and cranny of his body. He had been researching the Callahan haunting non-stop since he had been introduced to Mrs. Callahan and the work was taking its toll. He had slept little, and his eyes were dry and bloodshot. His back ached from too much sitting in uncomfortable office chairs and even his hands were numb from all the time he'd spent hammering away at keyboards in front of glaring computer monitors.

And then there was the frustration factor. It wasn't that Chambers hated research. In fact, he loved it. It opened doors and windows to worlds he had known existed but knew virtually nothing about. He enjoyed discovering facts and unlocking mysteries. But he hated running into dead ends, and that's what the Callahan case had been from the beginning. The harder he looked, it seemed, the harder it became to find anything.

Of course, he'd had the breakthrough with the photograph of Janet Sutton. Janet Sutton, the teacher. Janet Sutton, the spirit who not only haunted the Callahan home but whom Chambers had had a full-on conversation with just the day before. How odd, Chambers thought, that he had spent most of his adult life hunting for ghosts, desperate to see one, to prove they existed (at least to himself) and then to have a ghost walk up to him and converse as though they were old friends. He shook his head in disbelief as he stepped into the museum's library. Oh, to re-live that moment, Chambers thought. *What questions I'd have for Miss Janet Sutton.*

The photograph, however, had proven to be only a temporary breakthrough. Although Chambers now had Miss Sutton's name and image, his research had once again come up against the proverbial brick wall. Poring through the library's files again, this time not only searching newspapers but public records like building permits and school documents, Chambers had discovered nothing new about Miss Sutton and the Jefferson Schoolhouse. There was no documentation past the date of the only photo they had. Nothing. It was as though the school … and Miss Sutton … had simply vanished into thin air.

After sitting awhile in the darkness of the county library, the glow of the microfiche viewer the only light in the entire building, Chambers had suddenly remembered the collection at the museum. *How stupid of me*, he thought. *I should have remembered this before.* There was an unsorted collection of photographs from the era in question stored in the museum vaults. Although it had been several years ago, Chambers had been through most of them—planning a special exhibit that, sadly, never came to fruition thanks to budget cuts—and he seemed to remember photos of the public pool that had been virtually next door to the Jefferson Schoolhouse. Maybe those would tell him something. *It's better than spinning my wheels here.* Chambers had switched off the viewer, locked up the library and made a mental note to call and thank his friend again for the use.

And now here he was in the museum, deep in its relatively small vault, dwarfed by ten-foot-high shelving units, their metal dividers sagging with the weight of hundreds of white Staples file boxes. Chambers wandered through the maze of antiquities and, as always, he was reminded of the final scene in *Raiders of the Lost Ark*, the scene depicting the vast warehouse and its hundreds of thousands of mysterious boxes and crates. Chambers laughed softly. When it came to warehouses, the vault in the Ventura Museum didn't hold a candle to the one that held the lost Ark of the Covenant. But, then again, Chambers knew he was no Indiana Jones.

Chambers wound his way back through the vault until he came to a section sporting a handmade sign reading "Photos" in black marker. He made his way into that area, brushing away cobwebs and hoping no eight-legged creature would go skittering across his face or get tangled in his hair, until he came to a unit marked (in the same Sharpie penmanship) "Unsorted." He followed the stacks of boxes, thankfully sorted chronologically, until he came to the single box marked "1890 - 1910." He removed the box from the shelf, surprised at how heavy a box of photos could be, and carried it to the workshop in the other room. He sat the box on the desk there, slipped into a pair of cloth gloves, removed the lid and started fishing.

The box was packed with manila folders, some of them marked with dates, most of them blank. Chambers looked at every folder despite the date, knowing that "Unsorted" meant unsorted. Most of the photos were re-prints, of course, but many were incredibly old and very fragile. There were photos of the streets of Ventura as they were at the early part of the 1900s, and of the buildings that lined the streets in those days. There were a few photos of the city's legendary pier, which at one point was the longest wooden pier in the world. And there were photos of people long gone. Chambers always got a little melancholy when he looked at photos this old, realizing that everyone in the photo was alive and well when the photo was taken but had passed on now, probably several decades before. *It's like looking at ghosts*, he thought sadly.

He had almost reached the last folder, fruitlessly, when he came to an envelope near the back. It was marked

"Public Pool, late 1800s/early 1900s" but it might as well have said "Jackpot!" Chambers eagerly snatched the envelope out of the box, took a seat at the table, and ran his finger under the envelope flap.

There were perhaps two dozen photos of varying nature inside. Many were reprints, many were originals. The first photo was one Chambers remembered from his previous experience. It depicted a group of workers standing around a dry open pit that would eventually become the City of Ventura Public Pool. The workers all wore what looked like blue jeans or tan dungarees (as far as Chambers could tell from the sepia-toned photo) and black ranger-type hats to keep the sun off their face and shoulders. Most of them had shovels in their grip, and Chambers deduced they had been digging out the pit behind them.

The next few photos were interesting but ultimately useless. They were photos of the Public Pool after it opened and were probably used in newspaper announcements or as publicity of some sort. The pool was surrounded by a tall wooden fence and a large sign placed there read:

City of Ventura

Public Pool

Open to Everyone!

Chambers placed those pictures to the side, thinking that they might be of interest later, when he could return to his normal life of running the Ventura Historical Museum.

The next photo froze his blood.

It was the original of the photo that he had showed the Callahans. Miss Janet Sutton, standing before a group of young boys and girls, her students, in a classroom at the Jefferson Schoolhouse. *What's that doing in here?* Chambers wondered. He picked up the photo and examined it closely. Although it was the original and over a hundred years old, the detail here was clearer than the newspaper photo he'd shown the Callahans. For the first time, he realized that Janet Sutton was quite attractive, despite the frumpy, old-fashioned attire and severe hairstyle, and he wondered what her lifestyle had been like back then. Had she been married? Did she have any children? Was she a happy soul or had she been miserable? There was no telling from the photo. Janet's face was blank of any emotion. It was just a moment of time, captured forever by the camera.

Chambers flipped the photo over and his pulse quickened as he saw the yellowed piece of paper affixed to the back of the photo. A typed paragraph stared back at him, and he read it eagerly.

"Archived December 20, 1955. Photo from the Jefferson Schoolhouse collection. Pictured are several unnamed students (ages estimated at 10-12 years old) and disgraced teacher Janet Sutton. Photo estimated to be taken in 1903 or 1904."

Chambers read the paragraph over several times. Jefferson Schoolhouse collection? He had never heard of such a thing, and he'd been over every so-called "collection" throughout the museum.

And "disgraced teacher." What did that mean?

Chambers flipped the photo over and over, wishing for just a tiny bit more information, but there was none to be had. He set the photo aside and moved onto the next one.

It was a photo of the Public Pool again, this time from within the wooden gates. At first, Chambers almost dismissed it as another publicity or newspaper photo, but something in the photo seemed strange to him. He peered at it closer, studying every square inch, when it suddenly dawned on him.

The pool was empty. There was no water in its tiled bowl.

He flipped the photo over, thrilled to find another yellowed square of paper attached to the back.

"Archived December 20, 1955. Photo of the City of Ventura Public Pool, drained of water, after the tragedy at the Jefferson Schoolhouse. Photo estimated to be taken in 1904."

Chambers sat back in his uncomfortable chair, his back flaring in pain, but he hardly noticed. *The tragedy at the Jefferson Schoolhouse.* What tragedy? What had happened at the Jefferson Schoolhouse and how did it tie in with the Public Pool? He tossed the photo on the table and spat a single word curse. Once again, things were becoming murkier rather than clear. He was concerned about the Callahans, and the escalating haunting. Hopefully, they had made good on their intent to get out of the house for a few days.

Chambers leaned forward and picked up the next photo in the folder. Another generic shot, tossed away in the later pile. Another generic shot followed that.

The third photo, though, changed everything.

Chambers stared at the photo closely, feeling the temperature in the room seem to drop around him. The blood drained out of his face and his pulse quickened. He studied the photo for what must have been a full minute, then flipped it over and read the accompanying paragraph on the back.

He grabbed his cellphone and dialed the Callahans' home number. There was no answer. Good. Maybe they were safe and sound in a hotel somewhere. He dialed Mrs. Callahan's cell number next, leaving a brief message to call him immediately.

He glanced at the final photo again and then stuffed it into an envelope and tucked it into his coat pocket. He stood, grabbed his car keys out of his pocket and headed to the front door.

He needed to inspect the Callahan home again, and he needed to do so now.

CHAPTER THIRTY-FIVE

What sounded like an explosion knocked Lisa Callahan out of the considerable shock she experienced as she stared down at the split-in-half apple imploring her to get out of her house now. She flinched, and saw that her husband did so, too, as the blast, or whatever it was, shook their home on its foundations, rattling everything in the cabinets and knocking photos off the wall.

"Kyle!" Lisa screamed.

"What the hell was that?!" Kyle cried, reaching out to steady himself against the sink.

There was another *crack!* and the house rumbled again, more paintings fell off the walls and crashed to the floor. Kitchen cupboards creaked open, and dishes inched toward the edges, threatening to dash themselves to the floor. The rumbling intensified and Lisa was horrified to see the refrigerator creep forward from the wall, the vibrations jiggling it away from its location.

"Mommy!" Lisa heard Keely cry, fear strangling her voice. "Mommy!!"

Lisa leapt up from the kitchen chair but was slammed back into it by what felt like an invisible palm to her chest. She tried again and was hit once more, this time with so much force it nearly knocked her out of the skittering chair. Lisa snarled. "Let me up, you *bitch!*" she screamed and this time she was up and free of the chair and running to her daughter's room.

Kyle was right behind her. "I'll get Luke," he told her. They ran down the hall, the deep rumbling seeming to grow at an alarming rate. *What is this?* Lisa thought frantically. *An earthquake? A plane crash? What?!*

She burst into Keely's room to find her daughter on the bed, her knees pulled up to her chest, her eyes wide o's of terror. "Mommy!" Keely sobbed with fear and relief. "Mommy!"

Lisa reached out to pick up her daughter ... and that's when the lights went out. It was instantly pitch dark and Lisa carried herself forward, scooping up her crying daughter and holding her tightly against her chest. "Mommy!" Keely cried. "What is it? What is it, Mommy?"

"It's okay, sweetie," Lisa told her daughter. "We're getting out of here." The continuing rumbling and crash of objects to the floor (Lisa heard dishes smashing in the kitchen now) made "it's okay" sound feeble, at best.

Lisa stood and looked around the room. But she could see nothing. Not only were the lights out, apparently, but the power was completely off. There was no comforting glow of a night light or digital clock to see even shadows with. Carefully, trying to keep her balance in the shaking home, she edged her way toward where she thought the door should be.

* * * * *

Kyle ran into Luke's room and nearly crashed into his son, who was racing out. "Dad! What's going on?" Luke asked.

"I don't know," Kyle told him, "But we've got to get out of here.

There was a long, drawn-out creak that ended in another splintery crash and the power abruptly went out. Kyle heard Keely scream "Mommy!" down the hallway.

"Dad?" Luke said, and Kyle heard the fear in his son's voice.

"Take my hand," Kyle told him, feeling the boy's fingers grasp his own. "Don't let go."

"Okay."

Kyle reached out and felt for the edge of the door. He found the smooth edge and pulled himself into the hallway, towing Luke with him. The hallway was dark, and the rumbling ground made it nearly impossible to negotiate but Kyle could see a little, thanks to the streetlight out in front. *Why does the streetlight have power and we don't?* Kyle thought absently. He saw the shadow of Lisa and Keely step out of his daughter's room and into the hallway. "Everyone okay?" he shouted.

"Yes!" Lisa replied. "Let's get the hell out of here!"

Suddenly, there was another crash, this one bigger than the rest, and Kyle felt the entire house *shift*, with a series of subsequent crashes and fatigue squeals. The rumbling increased a notch, like a car shifting to the next gear.

Then the lights were back on and, although they could easily see to move forward through the trembling home, the Callahans found themselves rooted to the spot.

Because every exposed inch of walls and ceiling was covered with the scrawling words, "You must leave this house now." The words were written not in the precise handwriting they'd seen earlier, but rather in the scrawl of a madman, and they curved and interwove and made an insane pattern of letters that covered the entire house in warning.

Kyle broke out of his momentary shock first. "Lisa!" he screamed. "Move!"

Lisa snapped out of it like someone had slapped her and lurched toward the kitchen. She was close enough to see that even the kitchen walls were covered with the threatening graffiti when her line of sight was suddenly cut off by something huge and heavy that smashed into the door frame there, blocking her exit way.

It was the refrigerator. The shaking and trembling had vibrated it away from the wall and it had rolled across the now sloping floor and wedged itself in the awning.

Kyle saw Lisa give it a push, but nothing happened. It was too heavy for her, and maybe wedged in place. She couldn't budge it. Kyle ran up beside her and put his shoulder into it, but it was stuck. "Luke!" he said. "Give me a hand!" Together they pushed and strained but still the refrigerator wouldn't move a fraction of an inch.

"God *damn* it!" Kyle cursed. He thought furiously for another way out, and finally decided they'd have to use the window in the master bedroom. He was about to share this plan with his family when he heard another sound over the rolling rumble.

It was a clicking, skittering sound, yet a sound with weight behind it. Strangely, he was reminded of the sound of sunflower seeds, of pouring them from a bag into his hands. It was a sound like hundreds of seeds, flowing over one another as they were transferred from one vessel to another.

And then Kyle saw what was making the sound.

Pouring from the doorway of the master bedroom was a *river* of bed bugs. Thousands, maybe hundreds of thousands, of the blood-sucking brown creatures, flowing into the hallway like a flash flood. Kyle's blood ran cold. He'd seen a lot of bed bugs in his career as a pest control expert, but he'd never seen … or even *heard* … of anything even close to this.

Beside him, he heard Lisa scream. He glanced over and saw her eyes with terror. She had seen the bugs, too.

"Kyle!" she screamed.

In an awkward burst of dark humor, Kyle wondered *What does she expect me to do? My equipment's out in the truck.*

"Luke, again!" Kyle said, turning his shoulder back to the fridge. Luke continued to stare down the hall, his face ashen. "Luke!" Kyle screamed louder, and his son finally forced his eyes away, turned and pressed his shoulder against the refrigerator. They pushed together. Nothing.

They tried to twist it and jerk it and shift it away from the door jam. It was stuck tight.

"Kyyyylllle!" Lisa screamed, and Keely screamed with her. Kyle glanced down the hall and saw the sea of bugs advancing; they were nearly halfway to his family.

"Come on, we've got to *move* this!" Kyle screamed at Luke. They turned and pushed again, both men straining and cursing under their breath.

There was another splintery explosion and the house shifted again. Kyle felt the floor heave and tilt under his feet. *Is this place going to come down around us?* he thought. But then suddenly the refrigerator was free, the last lurch breaking it loose from its wedged position in the door jam, and Luke and Kyle shoved it out of the way with little effort, calling "Come on, move!" to his wife and daughter.

Lisa didn't need to be told twice, racing behind her husband, holding her daughter close and running toward the front door, only slightly aware of "You Must Leave This House Now" neatly vandalizing every wall. She could feel bed bugs crawling all over her, in her hair, in her clothes, but she ignored that for now, all of her focus on getting to the front door and the getting the hell out of this house. The door was just ahead now, she could see it clearly. They were going to make it!

There was another huge crash and the floor seemed to drop from beneath her. Lisa and Keely fell to the floor, Lisa spinning in mid-air to keep from landing on her daughter. They fell to the ground in a heap and Lisa felt the air knocked out of her lungs. She gulped for breath, stood again, grabbed her sobbing and screaming daughter by the hand and ran for the front door. She could see Luke and Kyle, ahead of her, getting to their feet as well.

Kyle got to the door first, turned the knob and pulled.

The door didn't open.

Kyle tried again. Still, the door wouldn't budge.

"Open it!" Lisa screamed. "Open the door, Kyle!"

Kyle stood back, looking at the door jam. What was once perfectly rectangular was now oddly shaped. Like a scene from that old movie *Dr. Caligari,* Kyle thought crazily. The rectangular door was crushed in the damaged jam. It wasn't opening any time soon.

"It's stuck," Kyle said. "Back door!"

The family turned and started back toward the kitchen. Before they got even one step, however, there was another huge deafening crash and the house shifted again. Kyle watched in horror as the refrigerator in the kitchen suddenly dropped out of sight, and a huge dust cloud rose in front of them. The stove was next, then the sink and cabinets. The kitchen was being swallowed whole!

The lights went out again and they were once again plunged into complete darkness. Kyle felt a desperate panic creep into him as he turned and tried to locate the front door, but he could see nothing in the Stygian blackness. He gurgled a cry of terror and defeat … and then suddenly there was light! Blessed light! And he could see the door.

Despite the calamity around him, Kyle froze for a split second in nothing short of pure awe. The sudden light was coming from every one of the "You have to leave this house now" phrases written on the walls around them. They glowed as though there was some hugely powerful light, a sun perhaps, behind them, the words burning white hot in the darkness. It was terrifying and eerie and yet gave them enough brightness to find their way.

Kyle reached the door, lifted his bare foot and began kicking at it with furious intensity. His mind had shifted to survival mode. Nothing else mattered but getting out of this house now. It *was* collapsing around them, coming down around their very heads! He wasn't about to let it take his family with it. His face snarled up in a visage of animal fury and he kicked at the door again and again, the pain in his foot growing, certain he was breaking bones, feeling the hot wetness of blood dripping and splattering, as he kicked and kicked and kicked again.

The house lurched once more and tilted like a fun-house, items spilling off shelves and shattering on the floor. Kyle was aware of his beloved La-Z-Boy chair sliding across the room and crashing into the entertainment center in a shower of glass and splinters. Through all the crashing and rumbling and roaring, Kyle heard Keely sobbing and Lisa trying her best to calm her. He kicked again, his foot connecting with the solid door with seemingly no effect whatsoever.

Then Luke was beside him, God bless him, Luke with those goddamn silly motorcycle boots he liked to wear just because they looked cool and he, too, was kicking at the door and Kyle was sure he felt the door give now and they continued to kick, the pain of the damage he was doing to his bare feet beginning to take its toll when, suddenly, blessedly, the door burst open, cool air rushing in and Kyle was stunned to find Eric Chambers standing on his front porch, an axe in his right hand, the axe which he had used to chop the door away from the other side, screaming at the Callahan family: "Come on! Come on! You've got to get out of there now!"

And they rushed out of the house, Kyle pushing the girls and Luke through first, ignoring the flaring, searing pain in his shattered and bloodied foot. He ran out past the front porch while behind him there came a huge and explosive crash, a rumbling boom that dwarfed anything they had experienced so far. Kyle didn't even look back, but just kept running. As he ran, he was aware that his beloved front yard ... or the area where the front yard should have been ... was now only a ragged, gaping black hole that seemed to be bottomless, seemed to go on forever, down into the depths of hell.

Fucking gophers, Kyle thought crazily, following his wife, his daughter, his son and his new friend, Eric Chambers, to safety.

CHAPTER THIRTY-SIX

Lisa Callahan came out of the bathroom in their suite at the Crown Plaza hotel, her hair heaped up and wrapped in the white terrycloth towel wrapped around her head, wearing the robe the hotel had given her that she had decided was "like wearing a coat of heavenly clouds."

The morning sun shined gaily through the window of the tenth story room, and Lisa marveled at the difference between the warmth of that sun today and the coldness of last night's events. She tightened the robe around her and surveyed her family, so very glad they were all still with her this morning, but felt a pang that everything they owned was now with them in this room. Everything else was gone.

Lisa's husband, Kyle Callahan, sat on the bed in his pajama bottoms (patterned with the motto "I ♥ Beer") and a Motorhead t-shirt, watching the hotel's big flatscreen TV. *We had a TV like that,* Lisa thought. *But not anymore.*

Kyle looked up as she entered. "Hey, honey," he told her. "We made the morning news!" He beckoned to his two children, who were sitting near the window, playing a hand of Go Fish with a deck of cards the hotel had, again, provided them with. "Hey, kids, look at this."

Lisa sat on the bed beside her husband while their kids joined him on the other side. Kyle cranked up the volume on the TV.

"A Southern California family is lucky to be alive today …" said the attractive morning news anchor, her face taking on a look of sober concern. "…After their home was swallowed by a giant sinkhole." The camera cut away from the newscaster to show an aerial view of Neath Street. Lisa felt her breath catch in her throat. There, in the middle of a nice family neighborhood, what had been *their* neighborhood only the night before, yawned a gaping hole … no, make that a gaping *crater* … that had once been the property owned by Mr. and Mrs. Kyle Callahan of Ventura, California. There was nothing there now but the sinkhole. No sign of the house, no sign of the front or back yard, only a few broken, dangling boards from what had once been the backyard fence and a ragged, gaping black hole that looked like God had fired a shotgun into the earth and left this wound. The place was ringed with police and fire equipment now, their flashing red lights bringing an aura of emergency to the scene. "Authorities say the family escaped with no injuries …" *Except for Kyle's foot,* Lisa thought, *broken in three places.* "…and an investigation is under way." The anchor paused for a moment and Lisa knew what was coming. *She's gonna do it,* she thought. *She's gonna do it.* And, of course, she did. "I guess that's one way for real estate prices to drop," the anchor said, smiling with smarmy self-satisfaction and self-amusement. *Yep,* Lisa thought. *Dumb as a post.*

They were quiet for a moment, the four of them, as the enormity of what had happened to them—and their sheer luck in escaping just in time—washed over them. Keely leaned against her father and put her arms around him tightly. Kyle responded in kind.

Luke had another reaction. "I'm gonna need a new PS5," he said flatly.

There was another moment of silence, and then Lisa couldn't stop herself. She laughed, shaking her head in disbelief, and said, "We're going to need a lot more than that, buster. Everything we owned got swallowed up in that hole. The TV, the fridge, all of our clothes and food, the furniture. But you know what? That reporter was right. We *are* lucky. We're still all here together." Lisa's voice caught. "It almost wasn't that way at all."

There was an awkward silence and then Kyle slapped the bed beside him. "All right, superstars," he said, standing. "What say we get dressed and go down and get some breakfast?"

"Yay!" Keely shouted, and Lisa felt her heart warm at her daughter's good cheer.

"Yeah, I'm starving," said Luke. Lisa was also very proud of her son, who had put down his iPhone this morning in exchange for spending time with his sister.

They lost their house last night, Lisa thought. *They lost their home. And they're doing so well. What a couple of great kids!*

"Me, too," said Kyle. "I'm so hungry, I could eat a baby's butt through a park bench."

Keely thought that was the funniest thing she'd ever heard, laughing giddily at her daddy's naughty joke. Luke just shook his head. Lisa laughed under her breath and gave him a disapproving look. "Kyle," she said, reproachfully.

Lisa got dressed quickly, donning the clothes her sister had brought them in the middle of the night. The pants didn't fit well and looked a little baggy, but the blouse was cute, and fit her perfectly.

Kyle slipped into the extra uniform he always kept in the truck cab in case of a spill. He hated to go down to breakfast in a uniform, but he didn't have much choice.

Luke had on the clothes he'd worn the night before, including the blessed motorcycle boots, and was good to go. Keely wasn't even six years old. She didn't need permission to wear her My Little Pony pajamas to eat breakfast anywhere.

They were ready to go and almost to the door when there was a knock from the other side.

"Room service!" Luke said jokingly.

Kyle walked to the door quietly and peeked through the fisheye peeper there. Lisa watched nervously, hoping it wasn't another reporter. There had been several of them at the door already and it wasn't even … Lisa glanced at the digital clock on the nightstand … it wasn't even eleven o'clock yet.

Kyle turned and gave her a nod. "It's Eric Chambers," he said, "and his wife." He opened the door and greeted them heartily.

"I'm so sorry to bother you after what you and your family have been through," Chambers said. "But, if you have a few minutes, I'd like to sit down with you and tell you what I've discovered."

"We're just heading down to breakfast," Lisa said. "Won't you join us?"

"We don't want to intrude," Becky said.

"Not at all," Lisa said, stepping up to the door and taking Becky's hand. "After what you and your husband did for us, it's the least we can do." She paused and said seriously. "You saved our lives last night."

"I'm sure that's over-simplifying things," Chambers said. "But we would love to join you. Shall we meet you downstairs?"

"We are literally on our way," Kyle said. "Let's go down together."

CHAPTER THIRTY-SEVEN

Either Kyle Callahan had been absolutely starving or the breakfast at the Crown Plaza's restaurant had been particularly delicious. He sat at a table with his family and Mr. and Mrs. Chambers and couldn't believe he'd polished off not only a waffle breakfast, complete with eggs, bacon, hash browns and wheat toast, but half of Keely's pancake stack as well.

When they had all finished, Kyle gave Luke a twenty-dollar bill and told him to take Keely to the hotel arcade. As the children went to play, the adults ordered a round of cocktails—a bloody Mary for Kyle and Chambers, champagne for Lisa and Becky—and Chambers pulled a now familiar manila folder out of his briefcase.

"So, tell us what you found," Kyle said.

"First, let me say that we are so sorry for what happened to your home," Chambers said. "If there was anything we could have done differently that would have led to your not losing your home, we most certainly would have done it."

"No one is blaming you," Lisa said, reaching over and touching Chamber's hand comfortingly. "If anything, you saved us."

"I do appreciate that, Mrs. Callahan," Chambers replied. He settled back in his chair and took a deep breath. "I'm sure you both remember our teacher friend, Janet Sutton," Chambers said.

"I'm not sure 'friend' is the right word," Lisa spat. "That bitch tried to kill us. Kill all of us."

"Actually, I don't think that was the case at all," Chambers said, adding, upon Lisa's raised eyebrow, "Allow me to explain."

He withdrew a photo from the folder and placed it on the table. Kyle and Lisa leaned forward to examine it. It was the photo of the drained pool, taken from within the pool house gates.

"Please note that the pool is empty," Chambers said, flipping the photo over. "And, on the back, I found the following inscription: 'Archived December 20, 1955. Photo of the City of Ventura Public Pool, drained of water, after the tragedy at the Jefferson Schoolhouse. Photo estimated to be taken in 1904.'

"What does that have to do with us?" Lisa asked.

"The Jefferson Schoolhouse was built in 1893 and stood through 1904. It was located nearly exactly on the very property your home was built on in 1960," Chambers continued. "In 1898, the City of Ventura Public Swimming Pool was built next door." He tapped on the photo of the drained pool on the table. "*This* pool," he said.

"I still don't see the connection," Kyle said, shrugging and looking at his wife, who also shook her head in puzzlement.

"Neither did I," said Chambers. "But the fact that there was a *tragedy* at the Jefferson School House in 1904 and that it tied in with the draining of the City of Ventura Public

Swimming Pool gave me pause to think. What kind of tragedy would lead to the draining of a public swimming pool next door? And then, I found this photo."

He placed another sepia-toned photo on the table and tapped on it. Kyle and Lisa leaned in close to get a good look.

It was the last photograph that Chambers had found at the museum the evening before and, despite the fact it was over one hundred years old, it was eerily familiar to both of the Callahans.

It was a photo of a massive, gaping wound in the earth. A crater the size of a house, with no bottom in sight.

And it looked exactly like the aerial video they had seen on the morning news not two hours before.

"The Jefferson Schoolhouse was swallowed up by a sinkhole in 1904," Chambers said, tapping the photo again. "When the sinkhole opened up, it not only consumed the schoolhouse, but fissures in the earth split the bottom of the public pool next door and the water from the pool drained into the sinkhole."

"Oh, my god," Lisa said breathlessly. "You said it was a tragedy. Were the children …?"

"No," Chambers told her. "All of the children at the school that day were rescued before the sinkhole took it." He leaned close and looked into their eyes. "In fact, there was only one casualty: A teacher named Miss Janet Sutton."

Lisa gasped.

"She died trying to save the children from the sinkhole. And she did. She saved every one of them. Sadly, it claimed her before she could escape herself."

A light flashed on in Lisa's mind. "That's why she appeared to us!" she said wonderingly. Kyle looked at her, not understanding.

"Yes!" Chambers cried. "Yes! Remember? 'You must leave this house now.' She was warning you. She was trying to scare you out of the house because she knew the sinkhole was opening again! She knew that the house would be swallowed! She meant no harm or misfortune. *She was trying to save your lives!*"

Lisa considered this for a moment. "Why didn't she just tell us?" she asked Chambers. "She spoke to you, told you about the school. Why didn't she just come to us and tell us about the sinkhole?"

"A question I have pondered myself," Chambers said. "But, unfortunately, a question perhaps only Janet Sutton could answer."

Becky raised a bony finger. "I've thought a lot about that, too," she said. "And I've got a few ideas. Maybe she thought she *had* warned you, thought that her messages on the wall and other ... um ... *reminders* were enough. Maybe she feared that a direct approach would be ignored or dismissed and, remember, time was a factor here." She took a quick sip of water. "Or maybe, for whatever reason, she was incapable of speaking directly with you."

"The sad fact is that we'll probably never know," Chambers said.

"This is what I don't understand," Kyle said, shaking his head and closing his eyes in confusion. "If what you say is true, if an entire school was swallowed up by a sinkhole, even in 1904, why was there nothing in the newspapers about it? Why couldn't you find any record of what happened to that school?"

"That was a big part of the puzzle," Chambers replied. "But then I found this." He placed another photo on the table. It was the photo of Janet Sutton and the classroom with her students.

"We've seen that photo," Kyle said.

"Not this one," Chambers corrected. "I found this photo last night during my research at the museum. It is the original of the photo you saw. On the back, I found the following inscription." Once again, he read from the tag directly: "Archived December 20, 1955. Photo from the Jefferson Schoolhouse collection. Pictured are several unnamed students (ages estimated at 10-12 years old) and disgraced teacher Janet Sutton. Photo estimated to be taken in 1903 or 1904."

"Disgraced?" Lisa asked.

"Precisely!" Chambers said excitedly, tapping the air with his finger. "'Disgraced.' And why was Janet Sutton a disgraced teacher?"

Kyle shot a glance at Lisa. Her return expression told him she had no idea either.

"I found that part of the story to be the most difficult to uncover," Chambers said. "But once I did, it became very clear as to why." He withdrew another photograph from the briefcase and set it on the table. It was one of the generic photos of the City of Ventura Public Pool House. "These photos were all archived in 1955," Chambers told them, "By a docent at the time whose name was June Dudley." He turned the photo over and pointed to the bottom of the attached tag. There, in tiny letters, were handwritten the words: "Archived by June Dudley, December 1955."

"Mrs. Dudley is 85 years old now, but alive and well and, I can tell you, a very sharp woman for her advanced age. I know, because I had a lovely chat with her this morning at her home on Loma Vista. And she told me the very sordid tale of Miss Janet Sutton."

The cocktails arrived and everybody was glad to get them. They took a moment to enjoy their first sips and then Chambers continued. "Sadly, Miss Sutton, an attractive single woman, as you can see from her photo, was the victim of unwanted sexual advances by a high-placed and very married politician of the time. Upon her rebuff, this politician took his revenge by destroying Miss Sutton's reputation and good name. He spread vicious rumors about her, about her sexual promiscuity and her inappropriateness as a schoolteacher. Unfortunately, back in 1903 or 1904, there was very little recourse for a woman in Miss Sutton's position, and she was prepared to do the only thing she could do: Pick up and move to another town to start anew. Unfortunately, before she got that opportunity to begin again, the Jefferson Schoolhouse sinkhole appeared, taking her life." Chambers had another sip of his bloody Mary. "These really are excellent, aren't they? Just spicy enough."

"I'm still confused," Lisa admitted. "How did that lead to there being no record of the Jefferson School sinkhole?"

"You must remember it was 1903, Mrs. Callahan," Chambers explained. "People were still deeply religious and superstitious. Their children were almost killed, swallowed up by what they called 'The Devil's Cavern.' They blamed Miss Sutton and her supposed promiscuity for the disaster at the school, much like modern so-called men of God say that homosexuality is the cause of hurricanes and earthquakes. They believed that Miss Sutton's godlessness was the reason that the town was punished by the near death of their children. And they decided to cover it up. To bury it, both literally and figuratively. They filled the sink-hole, paved it over, and Neath Street was born. All records of the tragedy were altered or destroyed. We were lucky to find what we did."

"How could they blame her?" Lisa asked. "She saved their children. Sounds to me like she was the real victim."

"She was," Chambers agreed. "But the lies of the politician weren't uncovered until years later."

"That's a very sad story," Lisa said. She raised her champagne glass to her lips but did not drink.

"It is indeed," Chambers said. "Albeit a fascinating one."

Kyle stared down at his barely touched Bloody Mary. "She was right," he said after a moment. "We had to leave that house and we had to leave it now."

"If she hadn't warned us," Lisa added, "We'd all be dead."

Chambers nodded. "Yes. The sinkhole would have swallowed you and your home just like it did the Schoolhouse in 1904," he said. "The ghost of Janet Sutton saved your lives."

CHAPTER THIRTY-EIGHT

It was Saturday, one year after the sinkhole had swallowed the home they had shared on Neath Street, and Lisa and Kyle Callahan were again both in their pajamas (Kyle sporting "I ♥ Beer" with pride), sitting in their new kitchen and enjoying the morning quiet. The kids were still in their beds, sound asleep, and this was grown-up time. Lisa loved it. Coffee, newspapers, and small talk. The best part of the day.

"I never wanted to live in a two-story house," Lisa told her husband. "But it's much quieter down here when the kids are up there." She took another sip of her coffee and broke a corner off the Pop-Tart on Kyle's plate, popping it into her mouth.

"Get your own damn Pop-Tarts," Kyle teased. He folded his paper and put it on the table. "Actually, you can have these. I didn't realize they were Brown Sugar. I don't like Brown Sugar. I like the raspberry ones."

"Poor baby.".

An electric *ping* stabbed through the morning calm. Kyle picked up his cell phone, glanced at the screen, and smiled. He pecked out a quick reply and sent it.

"Who was that? Lisa asked.

"Eddie," Kyle told her. "Wanted to know if we're still on for Taco Tuesday."

"Well, we are, aren't we?"

"Of course, we are," Kyle said. "It's Taco Tuesday."

He stood and walked over to the refrigerator. He liked the new fridge better. It had an icemaker built into the door and the freezer was on the bottom where it should be. He liked the new stove better, too. No visible burners and much easier to clean. Hell, he liked this whole house better. As much as he missed the house on Neath, he had to admit this house was better all the way around. *If your house gets swallowed up by Satan's Sinkhole*, Kyle mused, *Might as well trade up.* Their insurance company had paid a substantial sum for the loss of the Neath home, after being embarrassed in the press for first refusing to pay by trying to play off the incident as "an act of God."

Kyle opened the new refrigerator and looked inside. The usual stuff was there: Milk, cheese, butter. Probably sixteen cans of various soda brands. Lettuce in the crisper on the left; craft beers in the crisper on the right. A package of hamburger; some Oscar Mayer Cheese Dogs (made with turkey and chicken and pork and pasteurized cheese product, according to the label), a half-empty bottle of Tapatio hot sauce.

And there, on the top shelf, sitting all alone: A single red apple.

Kyle felt his heart skip a beat.

"Honey," he asked, not taking his eyes off the shining, red fruit. "Is this your apple?"

There was a brief pause before she answered: "What apple?" and Kyle could hear her nervousness.

He reached in and grabbed the apple, marveled at what a *good* apple it seemed to be. The color was right, the fruit was firm. It looked like a really delicious apple. But what would happen if he cut that apple? What would happen if he took a knife and split it down the middle? What would it reveal this time?

"Where'd you get that?" Lisa asked, seeing the apple in Kyle's hand. Her eyes widened.

"Top shelf," Kyle replied. "Sitting there all by itself."

"Don't eat it," Lisa said. "Don't cut it."

"Lisa, it's an apple. It can't hurt us."

"Please, Kyle," Lisa said. "Don't cut it."

"It's just an apple, honey," Kyle said again, opening a drawer and removing a knife. "It's just an apple."

He set the apple on the table and ran the knife through its center, feeling a little guilty as his wife gasped when the sides fell apart. The white meat of the apple faced up toward the ceiling, its five-pointed star staring up from the center of each slice.

Kyle felt his body relax. *Just an apple*, he thought.

Suddenly, from the kitchen doorway, came the voice of the demon.

"Hey," Luke said angrily. "That's *my* apple!"

And he stared in indignant confusion as his parents laughed hysterically and uncontrollably.

ABOUT THE AUTHOR

R. Scott Bolton lives in Ventura with his wife Shelley, his son Josh and his dogs, Zoey and Pretzel. He hosts a number of podcasts just for fun, and reviews movies and television as Scott the Video Guy on AM 1590 KVTA out of Ventura. For more information, please visit the website at rscottbolton.com.

Scott loves to hear from readers and welcomes e-mails at rsb@rscottbolton.com.

Made in the USA
Middletown, DE
27 September 2022

11162026R00181